WEREWOLF ART THOU?

A PARANORMAL MYSTERY ADVENTURE

MONSTERS OF JELLYFISH BEACH 5

WARD PARKER

MAD MANGROVE MEDIA, LLC

CONTENTS

CHAPTER 1
UP IN SMOKE

"It must come from your gut," Angela instructed me.

"It *is* coming from my gut," I replied, grunting. "I'm about to give myself a hernia."

It was a peaceful evening in Angela's upscale Jellyfish Beach neighborhood, and I was attempting to levitate an elephant. What else would I be doing on a Sunday night?

You see, I was visiting Angela for my weekly magic lessons. The powerful mage, a title reserved for the highest level of witches, had finally forgiven me for briefly suspecting her in the murder of a voodoo sorcerer (long story). We had resumed my lessons, for which she accepted no payment other than an expensive bottle of single malt Scotch every week.

Percy, the elephant with human intelligence thanks to voodoo genetic editing, had escaped yet again from the safari park where he lived. He was smitten with me and, somehow, found me here at Angela's. Fortunately, he had rudimentary magic skills that allowed him to travel here without being seen by humans.

Angela had told him that, if he was going to keep interrupting our lessons, we might as well use him in them.

Hence, my assignment was to levitate the 10,000-pound pachyderm. And I swear he'd gained a few hundred pounds since I saw him last. Life was easy at the safari park where he lived.

My love for you, babe, makes your magic strong enough to raise my body above the earth, he said to me telepathically.

"Nonsense," Angela said, having heard his flirting. "Missy was born with nascent telekinetic powers. She's never fully developed them. Only magic—not your puppy love—can allow her to reach her full potential."

All I am, then, is a prop?

"When you show up uninvited, yes," Angela replied.

She seemed a bit too rude to me, but Angela took her magic very seriously. In fact, it had saved her life on many occasions. Hopefully, she hadn't hurt Percy's feelings.

Anything I can do to help, he said sarcastically.

So, here we were in Angela's backyard on the shore of beautiful Lake Algae, multi-million-dollar homes beside us and facing us across the palm-tree-lined waters. And I was lifting an elephant into the air.

Telekinesis had never been a necessary tool for my magic. I discovered I had the ability when I hit adolescence but used it for little more than party tricks, such as bending spoons or stopping the fall of an accidentally dropped object. This was before I learned I had the magic gene.

I had mastered the ability to load and unload my dishwasher with my mind alone, but, frankly, it was faster to do it by hand. As my magic skills improved, I used my telekinesis only to enhance certain spells.

When Angela learned I was telekinetic, she was more excited about it than I was.

"On its own, your telekinesis can only move inanimate objects and cooperative creatures like this elephant. But to create truly powerful magic, you must harvest every drop of energy available to you," she had said. "That's why your natural paranormal abilities need to be fully strengthened and developed."

Therefore, with my mind alone and without any magic, I lifted Percy in the air in Angela's backyard, between her swimming pool and her dock. It was essentially strength training, like lifting weights. Up and down, up and down, in three sets of eight reps.

Straining my mind, I lifted him above the top of the cocoplum hedge along Angela's property line. This would have exposed the floating elephant to her neighbors had he not made himself invisible to them.

Angela and I could see Percy, though. His lovesick eyes filling with anxiety as he rose into the air.

"Do you smell that smoke?" Angela asked. "It's not firewood smoke."

It was winter, and in South Florida, whenever it dipped below 75 degrees Fahrenheit, it was fireplace weather. But Angela was correct. This odor was not a burning log or even that fake firewood.

It had the toxic odor of paint, metal, plastic, and other substances, including wood.

In short, someone's house was on fire.

"Over there," Angela said, pointing. "It's someone in my neighborhood."

A column of dark smoke rose from a point along the lake south of here. Her immediate neighbors' homes blocked our view of the actual house.

Angela's backyard trembled from a large impact, followed by an angry trumpeting.

"Oops. Sorry, Percy," I said.

The fire had distracted me, breaking my telekinetic hold on Percy and dropping him to the ground.

I am only a dumbbell to you.

"No," I replied. "You're a sweet friend. And the only five-ton object here for me to lift."

"I'm going to see whose house is on fire and if they need help," Angela said. "You can come with me if you want."

We jogged around the side of her house and got into her giant Cadillac from another era. She drove through this older but expensive neighborhood toward the billowing smoke. I heard sirens approaching.

The road curved sharply to the left, and there the house was directly in front of us, the second story engulfed in flames. It was a new home, having replaced a smaller, older one that had been knocked down. Built in a modern style that I found showy and unattractive, it was also, apparently, highly flammable.

Small groups of neighbors watched the blaze from safe distances, but the first responders weren't here yet. Angela pulled up right in front of the house, jumped out of the car, and raced to the front door. I'd never seen anyone move so fast into danger, especially not a librarian in her seventies.

She tried the front door, but it was locked. She rang the doorbell and pounded on the door.

"Is anyone in there?" she shouted. "I'm coming in to help!"

She must have cast a spell to unlock the door because she yanked it open, causing us to be hit by a wall of dark smoke.

Angela disappeared into the smoke. I was right behind her, casting a protection spell for myself, though I wasn't sure if it would protect me from flames.

An explosion of glass shattering erupted above me right before I went inside. All the upstairs windows blew out. Then, the downstairs windows did, too.

I couldn't see Angela because the smoke was too thick. I heard her calling out, asking if anyone needed help.

Her voice sounded like it was ascending to the upstairs.

A hand grabbed my shoulder from behind. I screamed.

"Get out, now!" shouted the firefighter, wearing a face shield and oxygen mask beneath his helmet.

"My friend is going upstairs, looking for victims," I said, the smoke searing my throat. Even my protection spell couldn't withstand the smoke and heat. I stumbled outside in a panic about Angela.

Another firefighter entered the house, searching for victims, while others held fire hoses, aiming at the heart of the fire. A mechanized ladder rose above the house with a nozzle that shot water into the upper windows.

Angela emerged from the house and walked slowly over to me. Her face was covered with soot, and her hair was singed, but she looked fine.

"Are you okay?" I asked.

"My magic protected me. I couldn't find anyone inside

except for one person. Dead. I couldn't tell who it was, or whether it was male or female, before the firefighters kicked me out."

"Why did you take such a risk going in there?"

"Because I knew my magic would protect me, if only for a short period. And because I suspected this was arson and a murder attempt."

"How in the world could you tell? With a spell?"

"No. Because this home belongs to Pierre Dunott. A city commissioner. And the most hated person in Jellyfish Beach. Well, I was right. Someone died in there."

"Did you honestly think you could save him?"

"I knew the chances were very slim. But I had another reason to go in. I wanted to sense if magic was involved in this fire. And the answer is no. The fire wasn't caused by black magic and not by a dragon or other supernatural creature. Finally, a death of a human that the Friends of Cryptids Society doesn't have to get involved in."

Little did she know she was wrong about that.

ANGELA and I were forced to stand with the other neighbors behind yellow tape, far from the destroyed home. Matt had arrived and used his press pass to venture onto the property to pester the firefighters and cops.

From my vantage point, it appeared that the first responders were strongly encouraging Matt to go away, but they didn't know him like I did. Try telling a mosquito to leave you alone without swatting it.

After the fire was completely extinguished, the home now a blackened, smoldering husk, the first responders and onlookers began leaving. Only then did Matt make his way to Angela and me.

"They can't confirm it yet, but they're pretty sure the deceased was Pierre Dunott," Matt told us. "They also said it was arson because they found traces that an accelerant was used—most likely gasoline."

"That confirms that the supernatural world was not involved," Angela said.

Matt nodded. "The question the medical examiner needs to answer is whether Dunott died in his sleep from smoke inhalation or the fire itself. Or if he was murdered beforehand."

After Angela had said Dunott was the most-hated man in Jellyfish Beach, she had explained to me why. He abused his power as a city commissioner to retaliate against local business owners who had once supported him but switched their allegiance to Dunott's political rival. By "support," she meant not just their votes in a recent election but oodles of campaign contributions which were now cut off.

In response, Dunott harassed them incessantly by ordering the police to pursue alleged code violations, revoking permits, even sending thugs to disrupt their operations.

"Do you think any of the business owners he harassed are responsible?" I asked Matt.

"That's exactly what I think. Dunott's behavior was reported to the commission, and they were supposedly investigating it. So were the police. But nothing was done to right the wrongs." He glanced behind him at the ruins of the house. "Until now."

"He didn't deserve the death penalty," Angela said.

"No, he didn't," Matt replied. "But apparently, someone believed he did."

MATT CALLED ME A DAY LATER.

"I heard from my source at the medical examiner's office. They believe the body was Dunott's. Also, he didn't have smoke stains inside his nostrils or signs of smoke inhalation in his lungs. No carbon monoxide in his blood, either."

"Does that mean he was dead before the fire?" I asked.

"I believe so. The M.E.'s office says there are rare cases in which the fire can be so hot and spread so fast that the victim's lungs seal themselves, and the person dies before inhaling any smoke. The fact that there was an accelerant backs up that theory. But I'm not so sure."

"Did they find any other possible cause of death?"

"The fire made that very difficult to determine. It looks like the body had penetration wounds, but we won't know for sure about that until the autopsy. We also need to see what the toxicology reports say when they come back, in case he was poisoned."

"Let me know if you learn anything," I said. This case was interesting to me because I had been personally on the scene. Thankfully, however, no cryptids or other supernatural creatures were involved. I was a mere spectator with no skin in the game.

Talk about self-deluded.

Two days after the fire, my doorbell rang at 5:35 a.m. My intuition told me who was at the door, and my intuition was right.

"We must download you immediately," Mrs. Lupis said.

"It is of utmost importance," added Mr. Lopez.

"Do you realize what time it is?" I clutched my bathrobe closed against the chilly morning air. Chilly for a South Floridian, that is.

"We apologize for not coming even earlier," said Mrs. Lupis. "We only now learned a supernatural species had been living in this part of the state, which is beyond its documented range."

"And now it's dead," her partner said.

"What kind of critter?"

"A loup-garou," they said in unison.

"A what?"

"It's a species of werewolf normally found in the French-speaking Canadian provinces and Louisiana, where it is sometimes called the Rougarou," said Mr. Lopez. "Some scholars call them high lycans. I call them bad news. They're much more powerful and dangerous than common werewolves."

"Really?" As far as I was concerned, regular werewolves were dangerous enough.

"Absolutely," he replied. "Even in human form, they're stronger and more difficult to kill than a typical human. They're often smarter, too. When they shift to wolf form, they're larger and more vicious than a typical werewolf. But they can also shift into a form that combines human with wolf.

9

They can walk upright on two legs and have human-like hands."

"Meaning they can use human weapons," Mrs. Lupis added.

"They also have more control over when they shift. They can resist shifting during a full moon."

"Wow," I said. "But if this one is dead, we have nothing to worry about."

My handlers exchanged looks of exasperation.

"We wanted to document and catalog it," Mrs. Lupis said as if speaking to a child.

"Right. Sorry you missed out. If that's all, I'll be going back to sleep now."

"That's *not* all," Mr. Lopez said. "Not for you. We need to find out who killed this loup-garou. Meaning, *you* need to find out."

"Why?"

"Because the well-being of cryptids is our mission at the Society, including finding out the causes and culprits when they are harmed. And it's your job to implement it. Was he murdered by another supernatural creature? Or by humans— most likely more than one—who knew he was supernatural?"

When I received the humongous grant from them, I knew there would be strings attached. As time went on, those strings became bungee cords.

"I see."

In that there had been only one alleged murder in Jellyfish Beach of late, my sleepy brain made the connection.

"Are you talking about Pierre Dunott?" I asked. "The guy who died in a fire recently?"

The two nodded solemnly.

"He was a loup-garou? Well, at least we now know that fire can kill them," I said, trying to put a positive spin on it.

Mrs. Lupis glared at me. "Normally, they can escape fire without injury or death," she said. "Only sustained immersion in flames will kill them. That means Mr. Dunott was already dead when his house caught on fire, or he was made immobile."

"What kills a loup-garous besides flame-roasting? Silver?"

"A silver bullet or blade to the heart will kill them. To restrain him in the fire would require silver chains or the right magic."

"You can't bind them with steel?"

"Strong enough steel will do," Mr. Lopez said. "The problem is getting him to be still while you wrap the steel chain around him. Silver will drain his strength."

That had been the case for Harry Roarke, an ordinary werewolf, when the Knights Simplar captured him, then pacified him by draping a sterling silver chain around his neck.

I pictured how the murderers might have overcome Dunott. I figured it would have been murderers in the plural to accomplish such a dangerous task.

"So, the murderers broke into Dunott's home and surprised him in his bed, shooting him with a silver bullet or binding him with a silver chain? I assume they would have to do this before he could shift?"

"If he was in human form at the time, they could have killed him with a normal bullet," said Mrs. Lupis.

"They could shoot and kill him when he was in any form," Mr. Lopez said. "But the bullets would have to be silver if he had shifted to full or partial wolf form. If he'd already begun to shift, forget about subduing him alive. I don't know if the autopsy will determine if he was shot or not before his body went through the fire."

"Why would anyone want to subdue him instead of just killing him?"

"To make him suffer," Mrs. Lupis said.

Wow, I thought. Dunott must have really known how to make people hate him.

Later that morning, Matt called. He confirmed Dunott had a talent for inspiring hatred.

"The business owners he harassed were at their wits' end," Matt said. "They tried to get the district attorney to charge him, but that went nowhere, especially since Dunott was reelected. Then they sued him, but Dunott's attorney has drawn that out for a year without a trial. They even tried to get a federal prosecutor to charge Dunott for violating their civil rights. It never happened."

"Dunott's victims must have been super frustrated."

"Yeah, because the harassment continued unabated until the day Dunott's home caught on fire."

The entire affair sounded barbaric, like we were living in the Stone Age. Then again, even the flowering of civilization hasn't changed human behavior much from that of our Stone Age ancestors when it came to bullying.

Matt had already written an article about the fatal fire for

The Jellyfish Beach Journal and was planning to do follow-up reporting. That's when I dropped my news.

"Are you serious?" he asked. "A werewolf?"

"A loup-garou. A scarier, more powerful werewolf."

"I wonder if the business owners knew that."

"That's what we need to find out."

"*We?*"

I explained about my assignment from the Friends of Cryptids Society and the fact that they believed it would take more than one person to subdue or kill a loup-garou.

"Not them again."

"Yes. They seem to be ever present in my life."

"Their assignments always put us in danger."

"Yes, they do."

Matt sighed. "Well, I'm going to dig a little deeper into Dunott's background, then I'll begin interviewing the business owners. I assume you'll want to join me?"

"Yep."

"We'll start with the owner of The Ripped Tide."

"I bet you'll enjoy that," I said. The Ripped Tide was a favorite hangout for surfers, artists, bikers, and assorted unsavory characters. Naturally, Matt loved the place.

"I don't know. Maddie is a scary woman. And she's not even supernatural."

CHAPTER 2
VAMPIRE DENTAL WORK

I would have preferred to visit The Ripped Tide during the afternoon when there was less chance of a bar brawl. However, Matt had to cover the Jellyfish Beach Women's Club Chili Cookoff, which, in our town, was big news. He said we'd go to the bar as soon as I closed the botanica for the night.

But then, I got a call from my vampire friend, Agnes.

"I am simply giddy with excitement," said the 1,500-year-old who had been turned when she was ninety. "A dear old friend of mine, Mathilda, has come to Florida to pay me a visit."

"That's wonderful," I said. "How long has it been since you last saw her?"

"Oh, about a hundred years, since shortly after we moved to New York. We left Rome to come to the US when the fascists took over before the Second World War. I first lived with her in a convent in Germany for centuries before we moved to Vatican City."

"Wow. That *is* an old friend."

"I'd love for you to meet her, dear. Especially since she needs some medical help. Dental help, actually. She cracked a tooth."

"Wouldn't her vampire healing powers fix that?"

"Our fangs heal naturally, of course. We wouldn't survive if they didn't. But this is a molar that was in poor condition back when she was a human. She can't heal it."

Being undead can do wonders for your health, except when it comes to the health conditions you had before you were turned. That's why I had so many patients when I was a full-time home-health nurse before I became a partner in the Jellyfish Beach Mystical Mart and Botanica. And it was why I still saw patients now and then.

"I'll take a look at it," I said, "but you know I'm not a dentist. I only know basic dental hygiene."

"I was hoping you had a healing spell."

To be honest, I didn't. "I'll look into it and let you know," I promised.

Having a four-foot iguana living in your garage has its drawbacks, but when he's a witch's familiar connected to you telepathically, he's invaluable.

"Yo," Tony said, strutting into the kitchen where I had just hung up with Agnes, his tail sweeping back and forth with each step. "You're looking for a spell to fix a vampire's tooth?"

"Yes. A broken molar that she has no regenerative ability to fix."

"How, exactly, did a vampire break a tooth? A fang would make sense, but a molar? Vampires don't chew on anything."

"It didn't seem polite to ask."

"It's unlikely she was munching on a mango and accidentally bit the pit."

"I highly doubt it. Do you know of any spells that can repair the tooth? Heaven knows, I will not go into a vampire's mouth and extract a tooth."

"No, I haven't memorized any human dental spells. But you know who we should ask? Don Mateo. He lived in an era when dental care was practically non-existent. Magic would have been the only way to care for their teeth, aside from yanking them out. If you were a wizard, that is."

"Good idea."

I summoned the ghost of the seventeenth-century Spanish wizard, who appeared, as usual, in my bedroom so he could peruse my lingerie drawer. He floated into the kitchen with pink panties on his spectral head.

"When are you going to tire of undergarments?" I asked him. "It's not a dignified look for a supposedly brilliant wizard."

"M'lady, when one is a mere ghost, one simply does not care how one looks."

"You got a spell to repair a vampire's broken tooth?" Tony asked him.

"Why don't you just pull it out? Assuming it's not a fang, of course."

"Nowadays, we would extract the tooth and put in an implant anchored to the jawbone," I explained. "I don't have the expertise to do that. Even if I did, I wouldn't want to do it unless the vampire was completely unconscious. I was thinking the right magic spell would kill any infection in the tooth and meld the broken parts together again."

"I have spells to stop teeth from aching," Don Mateo said, "to whiten teeth, and to mask bad breath, but not for what you're requesting."

"Come on, buddy, show a little imagination," Tony said in his gruff New York accent. "Don't you have a spell to repair a broken vase?"

"Yes, but—"

"But what? The concept is the same. Just adapt it for a tooth instead of glass or china."

Don Mateo harrumphed. "It is not as easy as you pretend."

"Pull your head out of your panties, and act like the brilliant wizard you used to be."

"Still am. In spirit, at least."

"Let's see what you got, big guy."

"Allow me to access my vestiges of memory. I shall return."

The apparition disappeared. I picked up my underwear from the floor.

"You didn't have to badger him so hard," I said.

"Badgers badger. Iguanas intimidate."

"Still, I thought you guys were friends."

"I knew him back in the day, when I was a witch's familiar stuck in the body of a Cavalier King Charles Spaniel. I'm just encouraging him to remember his legacy of greatness."

Don Mateo reappeared, sitting on the counter.

"I have the perfect remedy. It requires a potion and a simple spell." He looked at me. "I'll dictate, and you transcribe."

After I served as his secretary, the doorbell rang, and everyone scattered. The cats dashed to the bedroom to hide, Tony sauntered back to the garage, and Don Mateo disappeared to the Great Hereafter.

It was Matt at the front door.

"Ready to go to The Ripped Tide?" he asked with a grin. "It's Felons' Night."

"Felons' Night?"

"Yeah. Everyone convicted of a felony gets two-for-one shots. You and I can't take advantage of the special, but the place will be hopping."

"I have to say, the owner truly knows her customers well."

THE ONLY THING good you could say about this establishment was that it was authentic. If a set designer created a dive bar, this was what it would look like. And smell like. And, if you were foolish enough to order from the grill, taste like.

It was busy tonight, as Matt had predicted. The rambling one-story building was right next to the train tracks and had been a packing warehouse for pineapples and other local fruits in the late 1800s. The dirt parking lot was filled with motorcycles, pickup trucks, and cars that made my beater look like a Bentley. Loud country music poured from the open front door.

"You know the owner is a biker chick, right?" Matt asked, pulling me aside.

I nodded.

"Maddie is Asian. But whatever you do, don't ask her if she rides a Japanese bike. She'll get really mad. Maddie's a Harley girl, through and through. She's also Korean."

"I wasn't planning on making biker small talk."

"Good. She punched me in the jaw years ago when I asked her if she rode a Kawasaki."

I followed Matt into the dimly lit Seventh Circle of Hell. Two surfer dudes high-five'd him, but the rest of the crowd ignored us, thankfully. He went up to a table in the corner where a middle-aged Asian woman wearing a torn T-shirt sat with two stereotypical male bikers wearing leather.

"Hey, Maddie," he said. "This is my colleague, Missy."

"I've seen her in here before."

I haven't been here many times and must have stood out here because of my lack of tattoos and piercings. I gave her a little wave.

"Do you mind if we speak to you about an article I'm working on?" Matt asked.

She gestured for the bikers to leave. They jumped up and disappeared like nervous dogs.

"Sit down," she said. We obeyed. "Is this about Dunott?"

"Yes. I couldn't go without speaking to you. You were one of his biggest opponents."

"Victims," she said. "Me and Johnny next door were trying to do something to stop him, but Dunott was harassing lots of other local businesses who didn't have the guts to stand up to him."

"Johnny?"

"Yeah. Johnny. Owner of Billy's Pizza."

"His name's not Billy?"

"No. Why would it be?"

"Anyway, we just wanted to hear about what Dunott had been doing to you."

"It's no secret. We haven't been shy about complaining. Ever since I switched my support to McDougall for the commission seat, and Dunott won anyway, he's been sending the health inspector here, claiming we have roaches and rats."

"You do. A rat bit my ankle once."

Maddie waved her hand dismissively. She was petite, with short hair dyed platinum and tattoos on her hands and face that looked like they were inked in prison. There was something frightening about her.

"He regularly sent the building inspector here, claiming we had all sorts of code violations. And he sent the cops here practically every night."

"For the fights that break out all the time?"

"I expect cops to come for that. But not for parking and noise violations. He even had me arrested once."

"For what?"

"Threatening to kill him several times."

"Oh. I see." Matt glanced at me. "You must not have shed any tears when he died."

"I sure didn't. I must be the Number One suspect in his death," she said with great pride. "Assuming it wasn't an accidental fire. And I guess it wasn't because the police have interviewed me twice already."

"So, it wasn't you?"

I couldn't believe Matt was so bold in his questioning. Good thing I was being polite and quiet.

"Nah, not me. I would have picked a much more violent way to kill him."

"Really? What would that be?"

"Let's just say you'd be able to bury him in a matchbox."

"Who do you think killed him?"

"Another businessowner. If not, maybe his wife. Dunott

wasn't the most faithful husband in this town, if you know what I mean."

"I've heard rumors."

"If she divorced him, she would've gotten half of their money. This way, she gets it all, plus any life insurance he had. I bet you the police are checking her out."

"I'm sure they are."

"You know what they say: romantic partners are always at the top of the list of suspects."

"I hate that song!" bellowed a tall man with a shaved head. He strode to the vintage jukebox and slammed a smaller man's head into the machine.

Maddie jumped up and carried her chair to the jukebox. Though she was much shorter, she smashed the chair over the head of the song-hater. He collapsed beside the jukebox.

The entire bar was deathly quiet, except for the music.

"See? That's how you handle disorderly behavior," she said to us with a big smile. "No need to send the police here."

Laughter broke out, and the bar returned to its normal volume, which quickly overpowered the country music song that had caused the altercation.

When Matt and I left the bar, we found Detective Shortle in her car parked beside Matt's pickup. She lowered her window.

"Why are you guys getting into my business again?"

"What do you mean?" I asked.

"Jellyfish Beach rarely has a homicide, but whenever there is one, I can depend on you two snooping around, getting in the way."

"We're not getting in the way," Matt said.

"It's almost like you don't trust a young woman to be a

good detective," Shortle said. "Would you prefer I was an old, fat guy?"

"No. You're a much better detective than Glasbag," Matt quipped.

Shortle laughed. "God forbid he ever finds out we're dunking on him behind his back." She resumed her stern expression. "Look, anyone with a brain would look at the business owners Dunott harassed as suspects in his murder."

"It's been determined that it was murder?" I asked.

"The autopsy was today. The medical examiner's report says he was shot twice."

"Did you find the bullets?"

If so, I hoped they wouldn't be silver bullets. Silver would mean the killer knew Dunott was a loup-garou. And that would mean more work for me.

"No. Why? You must really believe you're an amateur detective."

I forced a goofy grin. "It seemed like the kind of thing to ask."

"I'm only telling you he was shot because it's what I was going to tell this guy, in his role as a reporter." She nodded at Matt. "You don't need to know any more. I've got this under control. And I'm warning you to stay out of my way."

"No problem," I said.

Shortle nodded then backed out of her spot and drove away.

"Little did Maddie know a cop was sitting in her parking lot the entire time," I said.

"I think Shortle is right. We don't need to be investigating this."

"I told you I was ordered to look into the murder because Dunott was a supernatural."

"So what? It sounds like he was killed while he was in human form."

"The Friends of Cryptids are very protective of monsters. And they want to know if the murderers knew they were killing a loup-garou. If the police catch the murderers before we identify them, we might never be able to talk to them."

"I can interview prisoners in jail."

"I'm simply following orders. I guess I'll have to investigate on my own now."

We got into Matt's truck, and he started the engine, shaking his head in frustration.

"What am I going to do about you?" he asked. "You make my life so complicated."

"Now you know what *my* life is like."

"Okay, we'll speak to Billy—I mean, Johnny—tomorrow. And any other business owners we think were harassed by Dunott. Are you satisfied?"

"I won't be until we find the murderers."

CHAPTER 3
SHAKEDOWN STREET

After learning that the owner and founder of Billy's Pizza was named Johnny, we learned that Johnny wasn't his real name.

"My parents named me Jonquil," he said, fiddling with his waxed mustache. "Who wants to spend their childhood getting beat up because you're named Jonquil?"

"I completely understand," Matt replied.

I studied the pizzeria, which was empty at this time of the morning. It was on Jellyfish Beach Boulevard, the town's main street, near the railroad tracks and next to The Ripped Tide. The farther away you got from The Ripped Tide, the nicer the establishments. Nevertheless, Billy's Pizza was a surprisingly clean, respectable pizzeria.

It was also a total cliche, down to the faux Italian decor that attempted to make it look like a cafe in a square somewhere in Italy. It resembled an illustration you'd see printed on a pizza box.

Even Johnny was a cliche. He looked like one of those small statues of a chef holding a menu board, a pudgy guy wearing a chef's toque, the waxed, black handlebar mustache completing the stereotype.

"Maddie called me last night and told me you'd dropped by," Johnny said. "And that you suspect that someone who was persecuted by Commissioner Dunott killed him. I thought he died in an accidental house fire."

"There were signs of foul play," I said after Matt introduced me as a fellow journalist.

"Like what?"

I studied his face to see if he was playing dumb. My truth-telling spell would have made these interviews so much easier, but the thing about magic is that it's never as easy as it may seem. Using magic to affect change in the world comes with a price. It takes a toll on me, exhausting my psychic energy. And it also disturbs the equilibrium of the world.

Magic must be used sparingly and wisely. That's why I would only use my truth-telling spell on someone we strongly suspect is guilty or is obviously lying.

"The police will release details of his death when they feel it's appropriate," I said. "In what way was Dunott persecuting you?"

"He constantly tried to shut me down. He claimed this place had code violations. Or health violations. He sent cops here all the time for noise complaints or claims that we exceeded occupancy limits. Nothing clears out a place faster than cops hanging around, especially late at night when a lot of my customers are drunk."

"He did all of this just because he was mad you didn't

support him in the last election?" Matt asked. "An election he won?"

"He took it really personal. I knew Dunott from way back, when he first moved here from Canada. We were buddies back then, and when he got into politics, I wholeheartedly backed him. With money, too. He promised to bring more parking spaces to downtown. But he never did."

"So, you supported McDougall instead?"

"Yeah. I mean, Dunott became a different guy. The political power went to his head."

"I don't understand why he kept harassing you even after the election," I said. "How could he stay angry for so long?"

"It wasn't just payback. It was also extortion. A shakedown. He collected money from all of us under the threat of even more harassment."

"Ah," Matt said. "That makes things much clearer. And a stronger motive for murdering him."

"I had nothing to do with murdering him."

"I didn't say you did. But if you had to point the finger at someone, who would it be?"

"Almost all the businesses along the boulevard were harassed by Dunott," Johnny said. "The high-end establishments closer to the waterfront were left alone because they supported Dunott. Most of the rest of us supported McDougall."

"But who on this block hated him the most?" Matt persisted.

"I don't know. People have their personal issues."

"Let me try again. Did anyone ever say, 'I wish Dunott would go away'?"

"We all did at one time or another. Why are you guys asking questions like cops when you're just reporters?"

Matt sighed. "Because we want to learn the truth. Our town deserves to know. Now, who should we speak to next?"

"Martha at Martha's Antiques. She was never shy about how much she hated Dunott."

"So is her name really Martha?"

"Yeah. Why wouldn't it be?"

Martha's Antiques should have been called Martha's Junk. Remember, we currently were at the seedier end of downtown. Her store looked like it used to be an auto repair shop, and her wares were scattered across a large concrete floor dotted with oil stains. There were plenty of dusty pieces of furniture from recent decades—items that were ugly even when they were new. Shelves along the walls groaned under the weight of appliances, such as grimy coffee pots and the first generation of microwave ovens sold in the US.

Martha was in the center of the store, haggling with an elderly man who wanted a faux-leather recliner. She was middle-aged, with a wide, florid face and stringy, prematurely gray hair. An air of bitterness hung over her.

After she sealed the deal, she turned her attention to us.

"Matthew Rosen and Missy Mindle from *The Jellyfish Beach Journal*," he announced. I always found it amusing that he thought I'd sound more credible as a journalist than as a witch and the co-owner of a botanica.

"What are you looking for? I have some antique typewriters over there."

"No, thanks," Matt said. "We don't use typewriters anymore. We're looking into the death of Pierre Dunott."

"The world is a better place without him, I'm not sorry to say."

"The police believe he was murdered before his house was set on fire."

"Too bad. I wished he had suffered in the fire."

"I'm sure his death was no picnic for him. Can you think of anyone who would want to kill him?"

"Oh, I don't know. Just about every businessperson on the boulevard."

"Man, this guy was a real winner," Matt said. "How did our town elect a guy like that?"

"My thoughts exactly."

"We heard he was harassing you like he did the other business owners."

"Yeah. He was always sending inspectors over here about building code violations. I mean, the wiring was a big mess, but I spent a lot of money fixing it. So then, Dunott started sending the police here on a regular basis, saying that I sold stolen merchandise. Next, he said I couldn't unload furniture while parked in the alley."

"This was in retaliation for your switching your support to McDougall?"

"Yeah. When Dunott ran for his previous term, I gave him a lot of fat donations."

"Why?" I asked. By the looks of it, this was not a profitable business.

"He promised to change the zoning on a piece of property I own and want to develop. That was a waste. He couldn't convince anyone else on the commission to vote for it."

"Has he been demanding protection money from you?" Matt asked.

"Oh. You know about that?"

"We've spoken with other business owners."

"Paying him was the only way to get him to stop harassing me."

Actually, I thought, killing him had been the only way.

A woman with two young children entered the store, so Matt and I thanked Martha and left.

"I get the feeling these business owners are going to cover for each other," Matt said. "If they know that one of their kind killed Dunott, they're not going to tell us."

"It's time to interview his wife. Maddie tried to cast suspicion on her, but even if she's innocent, she'll have a valuable perspective about who might have killed her husband."

"Last time we interviewed a surviving spouse, she wasn't grieving at all."

"Let's hope this time it goes as easily as that."

It didn't.

We found Georgette Dunott staying at her neighbor's home. And she was distraught. I had thought the neighbor, a worried, bird-like woman, would tell us to go away, but Georgette called out that she wanted to speak with us. The neighbor led us into the family room just off the kitchen.

Yes, the widow was grieving. But she was also supernatural. I sensed it before I even entered the room by the tingling in my scalp and forearms. She was tall and slim with sharp, delicate features and short black hair. I concentrated on the energy emanating from her. Shifter, yes. I couldn't identify what variety she was, but it would be a safe guess that she was a werewolf or, even, a loup-garou like her late husband.

"I'm so sorry for your loss," I said, echoed by Matt, as we sat across from her and made polite small talk, procrastinating on the hard questions.

"I'm glad you're here," Georgette said. "I want to get the word out in the press that Pierre was murdered. He didn't fall asleep smoking in bed, like some people might say. As far as I know, the police haven't announced that they suspect it was murder, too."

"I mentioned the possibility in my initial story," Matt said, "but I'll be more obvious in my next story if I can quote you."

She nodded and dabbed her eyes with a tissue.

"Pierre has already been unfairly treated in the news because of the false accusations those horrible people made about him."

"The business owners on the boulevard?" I asked.

"Yes. I'm convinced that they were the ones who killed poor Pierre. The detective seemed to suspect me at first. I suppose spouses are always the first suspects. But Mary and I were out of town all day when it happened." She gestured to the bird-like neighbor, who had been hovering by the door protectively. "We went down to Boca Raton to shop."

"Which business owner do you think is most likely to have done it?" I asked.

"That low-class woman who owns the dive bar was always the loudest in complaining about him. She also associates with known criminals."

Matt looked stung. I could understand that he was loyal to Maddie, but, really, she was the one I would pick as most likely to murder someone.

"What about the other business owners?" Matt asked.

"They could have been in on it, too. They could have chipped in and hired a hit man."

I didn't believe any hit men lived within a hundred-mile radius of Jellyfish Beach. Then again, I never believed before that Felix Carrascal, a Colombian drug lord, would own a vacation home here. You don't have to live and work in the same town.

"Did you mention this possibility to the police?" Matt asked.

"That woman detective was the one who brought up the possibility."

Matt scratched his beard and took copious notes. He seemed excited by this angle.

"What about someone else entirely?" I asked. "Did your husband receive any threats from the man he beat in the commission race, Stuart McDougall?"

"He never said he did. After all, it's just a seat on the city commission, hardly worth killing someone over. Mr. McDougall is a successful attorney, so it's not like he needed to win this office."

"True," Matt said, standing. "We've taken too much of your time during a traumatic period. One last thing. Did Pierre have an aide or assistant who helped him with his political work?"

"Yes. A young man named Greg Ackney."

"Do you know where I can reach him?"

"Oh, dear. I don't have his number. I suppose it's some-where in Pierre's home office."

"No worries," Matt said. "I'll ask around at the commission. Thank you so much for speaking with us."

After we piled into his pickup, I asked why he looked insulted when Maddie was mentioned.

"Not insulted. Just worried that she was involved. If our newspaper printed one of those readers' choice awards, her bar would win Most Likely to Be a Homicide Scene."

"You know, let's go talk to McDougall. He probably knows about more dirt on Dunott than anyone else. He might have some interesting suggestions."

Matt drove toward downtown and called McDougall's office, asking to speak with the attorney.

"Then when would he be available . . . I see. Thank you." He clicked off the call.

"They gave me some nonsense about setting up a time the week after next. These personal-injury attorneys never want to speak with a reporter unless it's to get publicity for a client."

"Why didn't you set up a time?"

"Because we're going there now. If he's in the office, I'm going to speak to the guy, whether he likes it or not."

The receptionist was not happy when we camped out in the waiting area.

"I told you he's unavailable now," she said. "Then, he has to go to the courthouse."

"I understand," Matt said, smiling.

"So, you're wasting your time," the dour old woman said.

"No. You're wasting your time worrying about me."

She hissed and took an incoming call, continuing to glare at us.

We waited for over an hour. The receptionist had a conflicted expression, as if she were debating calling the police. She picked up the phone, pressed a button, and whispered something.

I wondered if there was a secret back exit that McDougall had used to leave. Maybe he slid down a pole like a firefighter so he could rush to the courthouse.

A conservatively dressed woman came into the reception area. She was in much better control of her facial expressions than the receptionist was.

"I'm sorry," she said. "I'm afraid I must ask you two to leave."

Just then, McDougall had the bad timing to pass by on his way out. I recognized him from his commercials promising to get big money for people injured in car crashes.

Matt leaped from his seat and accompanied the attorney out the door and to the elevator, trapping him while he waited for it to arrive.

"Mr. McDougall, can I have a statement regarding the murder of your former opponent in the commission race?" he asked, flashing his press badge, even though McDougall had met him before.

"I only heard about it today. My condolences to his family. Now, leave me alone."

"Do you think he had it coming, with all the accusations about his harassment and extortion of business owners?"

"Of course not. I wish the state and the Feds had enough time to indict him. That's what he deserved."

With a "ding," the elevator door opened. But McDougall darted away to a nearby stairwell.

"I have no other comments," he said before disappearing.

Matt smiled at me. "See, that's how it's done."

"Being a reporter requires a certain, I'm not sure of the word."

"Persistence?"

"No. Obnoxiousness."

"Of that, I have plenty. Now, I want to speak with Detective Shortle about her hit-man theory."

CHAPTER 4
BUMP STING

We weren't far from the police station, so we drove past the parking lot to see if we could spot her car.

"Shortle is in," I said, pointing at the generic department-issued vehicle I had grown familiar with. "There's her car."

"We'll make sure she doesn't escape without talking with us, even if she's interrogating a suspect now. We'll give her the McDougall treatment."

She wasn't holed up working. She was sitting in a chair in the small lobby, chatting with the desk sergeant, a handsome man I didn't recognize. Detective Glasbag was there, too, leaning against the counter as if he didn't have a care in the world.

The detectives looked like they had nothing on their plates. You wouldn't think a city commissioner had allegedly been murdered.

Shortle's face didn't exactly light up when she saw us enter the building.

"I've got no new statements to make, Rosen," she said. "And what are *you* doing here?" she asked me. "There's nothing going on with the occult today."

"You ended your investigation of the blood, goats, and bats that invaded the hotel ballroom?" I asked with maximum sarcasm.

"It's ongoing. No recent developments."

My mother had admitted that she and her magic were behind the supernatural attack. It shouldn't be that difficult for Shortle to find incriminating evidence. You see, that was the problem with a world in which no one believed in magic.

"We're here to talk to you about the Dunott murder," Matt said. "I had hoped you would have sent me the autopsy results."

"I told you verbally. Why would I want to release the details to the public?" Shortle replied.

Glasbag grunted with approval and gave Matt a cocky grin.

"No, you don't have to," Matt said. "I wanted to ask you specifics about the gunshot wounds. Were there just two wounds?"

Shortle glared at him. "Probably two. It was difficult to say with the damage from the fire."

"Right. Any shell casings on the scene? What about bullets found in the body or in the room?"

"That is confidential while the investigation is pending."

"Would any of those bullets happen to be made of silver?" Matt asked with a mischievous smile.

36

"Silver? Are you saying Dunott was a werewolf?" Glasbag said, guffawing.

"No. Werewolves don't exist. But I do think he may have been murdered by a hitman."

"Where would you get that idea?" Shortle asked snidely.

"From you. You mentioned the theory to the victim's wife."

"You stay away from my witnesses."

Matt laughed. "Whatever. Is this hitman just a theory, or do you have any evidence of him or her?"

"No comment. Do you guys have any reason to be here other than pestering me? If not, I'd suggest you take your leave now."

"Have a productive afternoon," Matt said as we left.

"It doesn't sound like she has any leads on a hitman," I said.

"Nope. But I think it's a good theory. We have victims of harassment who have a motive to get rid of Dunott. But they're not of the criminal world. This doesn't appear to be a crime of passion in which someone snaps and goes against their nature to kill someone. If you were otherwise law-abiding citizens who wanted someone dead, you'd hire a contractor to do the job."

"So, you're ruling out Dunott's wife?"

"For now. Remember, she has an alibi covering the entire day he was killed. Unless we learn of a motive for her to hire a killer aside from the life insurance. From what I've heard, the Dunotts were quite well off."

"How on earth do we find out if the business owners hired a hitman and who he was?"

"Your truth-telling spell?"

"It wouldn't be practical to use it on every person in Jellyfish Beach. Besides, after I use it on the first person, he or she would be alarmed after blabbing so freely to me. He'd tell the others to stay away from me. Magic can help us solve crimes, but it can't do all the work on its own. It's unethical to use it without restraint."

"Your mother doesn't worry about ethics."

"Because she has none. She's evil."

"I have another suggestion about how your magic can help us. Remember that spell you used to spy on the Knights Simplar meeting when I infiltrated them?"

"Sure, my penetration spell for observing through walls. What do you propose?"

"I covered a murder-for-hire years ago in Mullet City. The police were wiretapping the suspects and used a technique called a bump sting to get them talking and incriminate themselves."

"Tell me more."

"You do something to make them paranoid. You get them to believe the police are onto them, or that someone else knows they're guilty and is blackmailing them. They'll freak out and talk among themselves about how to handle the emergency while the police tape their conversations."

"You want to use my magic for wiretapping?"

"As long as it doesn't go against your vaunted ethics."

I smiled. "It probably does if I really think about it. But this was a murder, and I guess I can push the boundaries a bit."

"Good to hear."

If I had to pick one place in Jellyfish Beach where hitmen and their clients would hang out together, it would be The Ripped Tide. Even Matt couldn't deny that. In fact, our bump sting might flush other, unrelated murderers-for-hire out of hiding.

The "bump" had to come from someone Maddie and her associates didn't know, so Matt and I texted it to Maddie from an anonymous account set up on a burner cellphone. This was the message we sent:

I know the hitmen you hired to take out the commissioner. $10K will keep me quiet. Send it here with a cash app.

Matt sent it while we sat in my car behind the building. My car wouldn't be recognized, while Matt's truck would be.

"If Maddie, or someone she knows, was involved in the murder, this will stir up the hornet's nest," I said. "If not, she'll just think it came from a random scammer and delete it."

Matt stared at the screen of the burner phone.

"Okay. The message was read."

"Now send it to the other business owners we spoke to, if you have their numbers."

A few minutes and several clicks later, Matt said he'd done so.

Now, it was time to do my witching.

With the spell Matt referenced, the one I used to spy on the Knights Simplar, I had needed to maintain contact with the wall of the hotel where they were meeting and basically send my magic through the concrete molecules so I could see and hear what was going on inside.

The present situation called for an alteration to the spell. There was no way I'd be able to isolate Maddie's conversations in the crowded, noisy bar. That's why I told Matt to steal some of her hair when he went into the bar earlier in the day.

"You want me to do *what?*" he had asked.

"Just get a few strands of hair. Surely, she keeps a hairbrush around somewhere. You might have to look in her purse."

"Maddie is not the type to carry a purse. She has a big leather wallet attached to her jeans with a chain."

It turned out that Maddie kept a brush behind the bar, and when she was in the storeroom, Matt had taken some hair from it, carefully concealing what he was doing from the only customer sitting at the bar—a fisherman struggling not to pass out.

Besides isolating Maddie's conversations, another benefit of this altered spell was that I could cast it from the comfort of my car rather than standing with my hands on an exterior wall of the building. That would be difficult to explain if someone saw me.

Because I couldn't use a magic circle in these circumstances, I relied on the extra energy from a magic talisman called the Red Dragon, which I now clutched in my left hand. The bronze figurine was the size of a lipstick tube and was molded to resemble a dragon. It had been left to me by my late father, a powerful witch. I never knew him. He had been killed as collateral damage by a demon summoned by my mother.

The Red Dragon was a copy of one allegedly owned by King Solomon. Let's just say it was pretty darn powerful, as the burning sensation in my hand demonstrated.

I gathered my energies, which were magnified exponentially by the talisman. Reciting the spell's incantation came next. Then, using the traces of Maddie's psychic energy left upon her hair, I zeroed in on her location in the bar. My magic concentrated the sound and light waves emanating from around her, until I could hear and see her, as if from a hidden camera just above her.

She was texting on her phone with her back to the beer taps. I zoomed in on her phone screen.

We need to talk, she typed. *Someone is trying to blackmail us about that matter.*

Who? asked the other party. They were identified only by their phone number.

No idea. Stop by so we can talk. Texting isn't safe.

I needed to maintain my connection with her, so I remained in psychic limbo while I waited for the other individual to show up. Matt understood what I was doing and kept silent.

After a short time, my car vibrated from the growl of a motorcycle engine approaching. The rider parked nearby and walked past the car toward the bar with a crunch of gravel.

I recognized him as a biker named Switchblade when he came into my spell-enabled view of Maddie behind the bar. He was friends with a couple of my werewolf patients at Squid Tower.

It wasn't surprising that he was involved in a murder for hire. He might even have been the triggerman.

He reached the bar, and Maddie poured him a pint of draft beer.

"Let's go talk in my office," she said to him. "Hiram, take over the bar for me."

Switchblade followed her into the storeroom where steel kegs were lined up on the concrete floor and wooden shelves were laden with cases of beer, wine, and liquor. A small desk wedged into the corner with two chairs must be her "office."

"So, what is this about?" Switchblade asked. He was a tall, muscular guy, covered in scars and adorned with tattoos. He fit the stereotype of a biker, except that he was getting up in years and wore glasses on a gentle face beneath balding hair. In fact, he looked more like a professor than an outlaw biker.

"I got an anonymous text tonight," Maddie replied, showing him her phone. "Do you think this is real?"

"It's not some scammer from China. They know about the dudes we hired."

"Have you talked to those guys since the job?"

"Nope. Last time was when I gave them the down payment. I'm still waiting for them to ask for the rest of it. I was thinking they chickened out and didn't do the job until I heard on the news that Dunott was knocked off."

"You gotta talk to them and find out what's going on. Who's behind this? They weren't supposed to tell anyone about the job."

"Maybe they're trying to dig more money out of you."

"Then I'm going to freaking kill them, too. I'm not going to be blackmailed. We gotta find out who's messing with us."

"What if it's the cops?"

"Then there's nothing we can do but keep quiet. I'll talk to my partners and tell them to keep their holes shut. And if your friends are cooperating with the police—"

"They're not my friends. I knew one of them from the state pen, that's all. He owed me big-time."

"If they're talking with the police, then they're dead. I mean it. I'll go freaking medieval on them."

"If they're snitching, you won't be the only one who wants them dead. And they know that."

Maddie and Switchblade were quiet for a while. Switchblade gulped his beer nervously.

"Are you wearing a wire?" Maddie asked suddenly. "Be honest with me."

"Heck, no! Are you crazy? Look for yourself."

He stood and pulled up his shirt to prove he had no hidden recording device.

Maddie nodded, and Switchblade sat down again.

"Anyway, the cops here are too dumb to pretend to be blackmailing you," he said. "I think our two guys couldn't keep their mouths shut about the job, and one of their lowlife friends is doing this."

"It's weird that they didn't collect the rest of their money."

"Yeah, but I'm sure they will soon."

"If they don't, I'm giving it back to my partners," Maddie said.

Someone knocked on the door, and the two stiffened.

"Who is it?" Maddie asked.

"Johnny."

"Come in." She unlocked the door and opened it.

Johnny, aka Jonquil, of Billy's Pizza, came in.

"Hey, I got this text," he said, showing her his phone.

Maddie glanced at his screen and nodded. "I did, too."

"Did the guys know about Johnny?" Switchblade asked.

"He was here with me the one time I met them," Maddie replied. She explained to Johnny the various theories about who had sent the texts.

"Could one of the other partners have sent it?" Johnny asked.

"Someone on our own team is blackmailing us?" she asked. "That's really low."

"It's also clever. They could send themselves the same text, so we'd never suspect them."

Maddie ran her fingers through her hair and sighed.

"That's freaking crazy. Switchblade, you go talk to the guys you hired, and see if you can learn anything. We gotta make sure this isn't coming from the cops."

Switchblade and Johnny left the storeroom. Maddie returned to her place behind the bar.

I released the spell, setting free the energies I had harnessed. Then, I downloaded everything I learned to Matt.

"Switchblade is right," he said. "Shortle is too inexperienced and Glasbag is too dumb to pull off a sting like we just did. It's a shame, though. They could have gotten audio tapes of these morons confessing they hired hitmen."

"Instead, all they have is my word for what I witnessed after casting a spell. No way that's going to be heard in court."

"We're doing this because your masters at the Friends of Cryptids Society told you to find the killer. I don't think they care if the killer is convicted."

"No, the Society wants to know if the killers are supernatural, and/or if they know Dunott was a loup-garou."

"Then," Matt said, "all we can do is find the killers. Somehow."

"I care if they're convicted, by the way. I just want justice to be done. Somehow."

CHAPTER 5
HITMEN

We waited for about a half hour for Switchblade to leave The Ripped Tide. He must have spent his time doing shots after he met with Maddie, because he was shuffling like a zombie on his way through the parking lot to his motorcycle. He straddled and kick-started it, sending a deafening roar into the night.

"I doubt following him is going to pay off," I said. "Do you really believe he'll head straight to wherever the hitmen are?"

"I doubt it. But what else can we do? Unless your magic will give us a solution."

"I'll remind you again that my magic doesn't solve crimes on its own."

"But it helps. It's like modern forensics. If you told Sherlock Holmes what science can do today with crime-scene forensics, he'd think it was magic."

Switchblade sped out of the parking lot, down an alley, and

onto Jellyfish Beach Boulevard. I followed at what I believed was a safe distance.

Switchblade wouldn't recognize my car. But it turns out he easily recognized that he was being followed. I guess a lifetime of being on the wrong side of the law gives you extra instincts for avoiding the police.

As we headed east along the boulevard, passing the businesses that had been targeted by Dunott, Switchblade kept speeding up and weaving through the traffic.

"Does he know he's being followed?" Matt asked.

"Yep. Thankfully, since his bike is so loud, I hope we won't completely lose him."

The shops along the boulevard were all closed at this hour, but the popular restaurants were still busy, making the traffic thick enough to slow Switchblade down. I thought we had lost him, but a couple of blocks ahead, I saw him ascending the slope of the drawbridge over the Intracoastal Waterway, heading toward the beach.

"There he is on the bridge," I said. "It'll be easier to follow him once we're beachside."

The narrow barrier island that faces the Atlantic Ocean had a limited number of residential side streets connected to A1A, the two-lane road that follows the eastern coastline along the entire length of Florida. In Jellyfish Beach, no passing was allowed on A1A, so if he took that route, it would be much harder to lose me.

After crossing the bridge, Switchblade rumbled eastward past the few blocks of businesses before the boulevard ended at the beach. He didn't turn onto any side streets. He turned right and headed south on A1A.

I thought I knew where he was going.

We passed the strip of beachfront mansions, hidden behind oak and banyan trees, and then condominium complexes began to appear. Up ahead were Squid Tower, where retired vampires had established their homes, and Seaweed Manor, which was filled with werewolves.

Sure enough, Switchblade slowed down and turned left into the Seaweed Manor parking lot. If I followed him into the lot, he would know I was who'd been following him, so I took the next entrance into Squid Tower, where I had a parking permit, so Switchblade wouldn't see me.

"We'll hang out here and give him time to go inside," I said. "Then we'll walk over and find his bike."

"And do what with it?"

"Place a warding spell on it. The ward will alert me whenever his bike moves."

"Who needs technology when you have magic?" Matt said.

"How are you, Missy?" asked the gate guard. "Here for a patient appointment?"

The guard was Bernie Burdine. He'd started working here a few years ago as a human who was unfortunate enough to be assigned the night shift. That went about as well as you would imagine, and he was turned. Now, as a vampire, he no longer was caught sleeping on the job.

"I'm just here on a social visit," I said, as he raised the gate arm.

I parked in the spot I always use when I come here for home-health visits for my vampire patients and grabbed my tote bag that was filled with my witch supplies.

"I wonder if one or both hitmen live at Seaweed Manor," I mused. "Or if this is where Switchblade lives."

"If he lives here, it means he's a werewolf?" Matt asked.

"Most likely. Now I wish I hadn't played it so safe. If he's visiting the hitmen, how will we know what unit they're in? Please search the property appraiser's site and see if Switchblade owns a place here. Do you know his real name?"

"I think his last name is Carbuncle."

Matt typed away on his phone.

"Ah, yes. A Sidney Carbuncle bought a place here last year."

"Sidney? Doesn't have the same ring as Switchblade. Anyway, knowing he owns a place here makes our lives easier. I assume the hitmen don't live here. It's not the most luxurious address, but it's a little beyond what lowlife murderers would choose for a home. Let's hope that Switchblade will pay them a visit soon. First, we need to look for his bike."

I got out of my car and went around to Matt's side where his door was open, but he hadn't budged. The hollow popping of pickleballs being hit came from the nearby court filled with vampire players.

"I don't feel comfortable being here at night," Matt said.

"Would you prefer to stay in the car? Would that make you safer?"

"No."

"Here." I reached into my glove compartment and withdrew two pendants on leather cords. Each pendant was a small pouch filled with dried herbs and powders, as well as plenty of magic. They were amulets that repelled vampires and werewolves. "Put these on. They'll protect you."

I wore them all the time as second nature, though the residents in the two supernatural communities here knew me and that they weren't supposed to prey upon me.

"Do these really work?" Matt asked.

"You'll find out, won't you?"

Matt groaned and got out of the car.

I led the way across the front of Squid Tower to a tall Ficus hedge on the property line. It had a gap in it I had used for years as a shortcut to Seaweed Manor. Once we crossed through, the condition of the landscaping declined noticeably.

You see, Seaweed Manor attracted a less refined crowd than the vampires next door. It was a party haven. A literal animal house.

I avoided the place during a full moon when all werewolves, except loup-garous, were forced by nature to shift to wolves. On any other night of the month, they could do so voluntarily but would usually leave the property to go hunting, which was forbidden here.

Still, I was in a stage of maximum alert as we walked toward the parking lot. I cast a protection spell around Matt and me just in case a hungry werewolf came upon us.

Heavy-metal music blared from an open window. Marijuana smoke wafted in the sea breeze. Matt tripped on an empty beer bottle.

"This place is like a college dorm," Matt muttered.

In the parking lot, I quickly found Switchblade's motorcycle. His bike was the only one with a human skull mounted on the rear "sissy" bar.

Making sure no one was around, I took a vial from my tote bag and sprinkled my warding potion all over the bike's engine housing. Then I conducted a quick ritual to cast the spell.

"Okay," I said, "the ward should notify me whenever Switchblade starts up his engine. I'll have to rush over here and try to find and follow him as he goes on the road."

"That's going to be a lot of work."

"I know. My guess, though, is that his priority is to visit the hitmen. I don't want to have to follow him every time he goes out for a cappuccino."

Matt snorted. "I see Switchblade as more of a cinnamon-almond-milk-macchiato man."

Footsteps approached us.

"Let's get out of here!" I whispered.

"Hey! Who's there?" shouted Switchblade. "Were you messing with my bike? I'll kill you!"

And he surely would.

He was too close for us to run away without being seen. Matt and I ducked behind a nearby car.

Heart pounding, I desperately tried to think of a strategy. The protection spell would keep us from getting hurt, but Switchblade would recognize us, and our mission would be aborted. Same thing with an immobility spell.

The easiest solution would be to incapacitate him with a sleep spell. But he was obviously coming out here to use his bike—possibly to visit the hitmen. Putting him to sleep would mess that up.

As his footsteps on the asphalt neared the car we were behind, I got an idea.

Using a very simple spell, I projected sound to the opposite side of the parking lot to distract Switchblade.

"Let's get out of here before he sees us!" I said in a loud

stage whisper, doing my best imitation of a male teenager's voice.

Switchblade turned his attention away from us and toward the projected sound.

Then, I scraped my feet and stomped on the asphalt to mimic a running sound. It came from the same direction my voice had come from.

Matt looked at me with a mixture of horror and bafflement.

"Get out of here, you punks!" Switchblade shouted, running toward the phantom sounds.

"He's distracted," I whispered to Matt. "Let's go!"

Crouching behind cars, we scampered out of the parking lot, over the grass, and through the gap in the hedge.

As soon as we got in my car, I locked the doors and turned on the engine.

"I've never seen you use trickery like that before," Matt said.

"Yeah. Less-invasive magic comes in handy sometimes. Wait, the ward just alerted me. Switchblade started his bike. Let's see where he goes."

I drove out the Squid Tower gate and waited at the edge of A1A. The ward was moving away from us, which meant Switchblade was riding northbound.

I pulled into the street and caught up with him. This time, I needed to risk getting closer so as not to let him out of my sight.

Switchblade headed north, then turned west, crossing the Intracoastal Waterway bridge. He passed through downtown Jellyfish Beach with Matt and me close behind. We whizzed past The Ripped Tide, which was still bustling at this late hour.

After crossing the railroad tracks, Switchblade turned north and headed up the street that ran parallel to the tracks. We went through a section of warehouses and offices, then old, one- and two-story apartment buildings. At the end of the next block was a low rectangular structure that appeared to be a cheap motel built after World War II. It probably once attracted budget-conscious tourists. Now, it was seedy, short-term residential rentals.

Switchblade parked his bike in front, next to a rusting car. I turned off my headlights and idled nearby, observing which unit he entered. Before he knocked, he pulled a handgun from the rear waistband of his jeans.

I pulled up across the street, and we waited, watching the apartment, hoping we didn't hear a gunshot.

Only fifteen minutes later, Switchblade left the apartment, kick-started his bike, and roared away. We waited a few minutes, then crossed the street to the apartment.

On the way, I gathered my energies and began weaving together a foundation for a spell. I didn't know which one I'd use, but I was sure I'd need magic of some sort.

"I'll play the tough guy," Matt said.

"Good luck with that," I said sarcastically.

He smirked, then pounded on the apartment door. It opened a crack, and a man peered out with one eye.

"I'm looking for Switchblade," Matt said. "He said he'd be here."

"He already left," the man replied. His voice was hoarse.

"We need to ask you a couple of questions."

"Go away, or I'll shoot."

I believed he was bluffing. So, apparently, did Matt.

The man pushed the door, but Matt's foot prevented it from closing fully. Matt pushed back, grunting. It was a standstill until I jumped into the contest.

Concentrating with all my might, I pushed against the door with my telekinesis enhanced with magic.

The door flew inward, knocking the man off balance.

He landed on his butt on the floor.

"Gun in his right hand!" Matt shouted.

Okay, maybe the man hadn't been bluffing.

Already cued up, my immobility spell froze him before he swung his pistol toward us. Matt stepped inside and pried the gun from his hand, tossing it on the nearby unmade bed.

"Just a few questions, and we'll leave you alone," I said, sprinkling the powder for my truth spell on his prone legs.

It was only then that I got a good look at him. I gasped.

"What happened to you?" I asked.

CHAPTER 6
THE CAT'S MEOW

The man, a slight, wiry guy with prison tattoos on his shirtless torso, looked like he had been savaged by wild animals. Deep gouges, apparently from claws, ran down his face, neck, and shoulders. A bloody bandage covered his throat. Another was wrapped around his side, just above his hip.

I whispered the incantation for my truth-telling spell, and his eyes lit up as it went to work.

I asked him again what had happened to him.

"A coyote got me the other night," he replied without looking at me.

"You must tell me the truth," I said as I pumped more energy into the spell.

"Do you believe in werewolves?" he asked.

"I do."

"Have you ever heard of a loup-garou?"

"As a matter of fact, I have."

He looked surprised. His eyes burned with excitement and the urge to talk, but they also held fear.

"We were attacked by one of them. He killed my cousin, Ivan."

Matt and I exchanged glances. He knew better than to speak when I was using this spell on someone.

"Where were you?" I asked.

"At the loup-garou's house."

"Did you kill him?"

"No. We were supposed to. We had silver bullets and were going to surprise him in his sleep when he was in human form. I was told he wouldn't be much stronger than a normal man if we found him in human form."

"Are you a werewolf?"

"No. But I'm afraid I'll turn into one now. Isn't that what the legends say? If I'm attacked, I'll turn into one?"

"Did the loup-garou bite you, or just claw you?"

"I don't think he bit me."

"If he did, you'd know. You'd be missing some flesh. If he only wounded you with his claws, I think you'll be okay. It's werewolf saliva that infects people with the virus and turns them into shifters."

I knew that for a fact regarding werewolves. My knowledge of loup-garous was lacking, though. For this guy's sake, I hoped I was right.

"Is Switchblade a werewolf?" I asked.

"I don't know. He definitely wasn't when I met him in prison. I didn't even believe in werewolves before this. Switchblade told us the target, Dunott, was a loup-garou to prepare us in case he turned into one while we were doing the job. Switchblade didn't want us to freak out and run away. But we failed, anyway."

"I don't understand," I said. "You shot him with silver bullets, and he survived?"

"We were told regular bullets would kill him in human form. The silver bullets were for backup. We only had a few, and they were in Ivan's gun. I opened Dunott's bedroom door and shot him right away before he woke up. Then I went up to the bed to finish him off if he was still alive."

"What happened?"

"He was still alive. And he shifted. But not into a wolf like I would've expected. Into a half-wolf, half-human. His bullet wound healed right before our eyes."

"Didn't Ivan shoot him with the silver bullets?"

"He missed. I loved my cousin, but I didn't know he was such a lousy shot. And by then, it was too late."

"The loup-garou attacked?"

"Heck, yeah. He went after Ivan. I guess he must have known Ivan had silver bullets. The monster tore him to pieces. I shot him two more times, but it was as useless as shooting him with a squirt gun. He came after me, too. I don't know how I got out of there alive."

"Did you set the house on fire?"

"No way. I was running for my life. I was lucky to make it to my car and drive away. It tears me apart that I left Ivan behind, but he was dead by then."

"What's your name?" I asked.

"Emile."

"Who hired you?"

"I don't know. A group of people Switchblade knows. He was the inter. . . innermed. . ."

"Intermediary."

"Yeah. He paid us one third up front. Tonight, he told me I could keep it, because—look at me. I need serious medical care. And I want to find a place to live in another town."

"Did you know Dunott was killed?"

"Switchblade told me. He thought we did it, but it turns out it happened a couple days later. I never talked to Switchblade because I was afraid he'd be mad at me for failing, and I knew he wouldn't pay me the rest of the money. In the end, he got what he wanted."

"Yeah. Dunott is dead. Only someone else took care of it for him. Let me ask you again. Do you know who asked Switch-blade to hire you?"

He shook his head. The truth-telling spell looked like it was fading.

"I'm a trained nurse," I said in a kinder tone. "Would you like me to look at those wounds?"

"Nah. I'll see a doctor in Orlando. I'm leaving here in the morning."

I thanked him and told him to change his bandages. Matt and I backed out the door.

"What did you do to me?" Emile asked. "Why can't I move?"

"You'll be able to in just a few minutes."

When Matt and I were safely in the car, I drove past the apartment. Through the open door, we saw Emile still lying on the floor. Only then did I reverse the immobility spell. I sped away in case he was tempted to grab his gun and take a shot at us.

"This is crazy," Matt said. "If this guy was telling the truth—"

"He was."

"You'd think the business owners used someone else to kill Dunott after Emile and Ivan failed. But Switchblade hadn't known they failed until tonight. And from what you overhead, Maddie and the others hadn't known either."

"Yeah," I said. "I guess Dunott was such a jerk that an entirely different party wanted to kill him, too. And succeeded."

"Maybe it was another person or people he was harassing who weren't part of the first group."

"How could a guy have so many people wanting to kill him and still win an election?"

"Things are crazy in Jellyfish Beach."

"Well, let's find someone else who would want Dunott dead."

WE DIDN'T HAVE to look far. We continued canvassing the businesses in downtown Jellyfish Beach, and it appeared that Dunott had gotten his claws into nearly everyone. Business owners complained about being retaliated against for having supported McDougall. Cash contributions to Dunott's "campaign fund" made the harassment go away.

But even owners who had no interest in city politics were victims. Dunott simply demanded protection money from them, like a typical mobster would.

"I voted for the guy, and still he harassed me," said Leticia Maldonado, the owner of a new Argentinian restaurant that had quickly become one of the highest rated in Jellyfish Beach. "He demanded a five-figure cash campaign contribution if I didn't want the health inspector to make daily visits to my restaurant."

"You're one of the rare business owners who voted for him," Matt said. "I did some research, and most of his support came from the wealthy residential neighborhoods."

"I'm fairly new in town," she said, "and didn't know of Dunott's reputation until it was too late. I refused to donate, and the next week, my restaurant was shut down for two days for improper meat storage, which was nonsense. Our kitchen is new and spotless, so that was the only thing they could think to charge us with."

"Have you heard any of Dunott's victims making threats against him?" I asked.

"No. Like I said, I haven't been in Jellyfish Beach for long. No one knows me well enough to say things like that in front of me. You should check with Fred Furman, the owner of The Cat's Meow. He's the leader of an informal club of business owners here on the high-end blocks of the boulevard."

Fred Furman was a neighbor of mine, living one street over. I hadn't known he owned a store here. In fact, I'd thought he was retired. There was one important fact about him that I did know.

Fred was a werewolf.

Fred Furman lived behind the three elderly ghoul sisters who were two houses down from me. Our neighbors, unaware the sisters weren't human, had nicknamed them the Golden Girls. When a UPP delivery driver was murdered in their yard, Fred improperly disposed of the corpse. He owed me big time for not reporting him to the police.

The fact he was a werewolf was a big part of my decision to spare him. After all, I hadn't wanted his true nature revealed to the police.

Another side of his true nature had shocked me. When I broke into Fred's home to search the place, I uncovered a room filled with a gigantic collection of plush animals. It didn't fit Fred's gruff personality at all. Nor did it fit in with being a werewolf. Since when did monsters like cute, snuggly things?

When we arrived at his high-end boutique one block off Jellyfish Beach Boulevard, we quickly discerned it was equally incongruous. The Cat's Meow sold cat accessories and cat-themed gifts. Many contained jewels and precious metals, but needless to say, none were made of silver.

"Fred, you're a werewolf. Why are you selling adorable kitten things?"

There was no one else in the store to hear me asking, and I had to know.

"I happen to like cats. Who says I must limit my love to canids?"

"No one. And I thought you were retired."

"I like to keep busy with promising retail opportunities. Are you here to buy something or to bother me? Can I interest you in a platinum kitty paperweight?"

"Wow," I said, looking at its price tag. "You have well-heeled customers."

"Yes." He returned the paperweight to the top shelf of a glass display case. Fred had thick white hair, including on his ears, and a couple of hairs fell onto the glass. "Jellyfish Beach is attracting the finest people these days. At this end of downtown."

"You mean not out by the railroad tracks?"

"Exactly."

"The reason I'm here is to ask you about Commissioner Dunott. Did he harass you in any way?"

"He harassed almost all the businesses, except for the ones he had a stake in, like the French restaurant on the water. He was like a Mafia capo, taking his cut from the rest of us."

"How did he harass you?"

"He had to be creative to find ways. This building was recently renovated, so he couldn't find any building code violations. This isn't a restaurant, so he couldn't send the health inspector here. So, he sent thugs to intimidate my landlord into raising my rent."

Fred was getting worked up. The short, chubby guy was red in the face.

"A thug would come by from time to time to collect campaign contributions," he continued. "If I came up short, he'd break merchandise. Like my adorable, jewel-inlaid kitty sculptures. I have some new ones in, if you're interested. I'll give you ten percent off."

"No thanks. Do you have any ideas about who would kill him?"

"Not anyone in the Downtown Merchants Association. We don't use guns to settle disputes."

"It's interesting that you knew he was shot. The news coverage has been that he was killed by arson."

"What are you implying? I knew he'd been shot because word gets around."

"The police believe a member of the local business community did it. One of his extortion victims."

Shortle hadn't let on who she suspected, but anyone with half a brain would have the same suspicions Matt and I had.

"I told you we don't resort to violence," Fred said testily. "I can't speak for some of the business owners, like a certain biker bar."

"The police already investigated them. Now they're focusing on your end of the boulevard."

I didn't know who they were focusing on, but I was attempting a crude version of the bump sting.

"Why do you care? You're just a witch and an occult-shop owner. You're probably a suspect, too. Dunott must've harassed you, right?"

"No. We're too far away from the boulevard in a seedy neighborhood. He'd probably be too afraid to come into our store."

In short, our clientele was not the type who would shop in a store selling jewel-inlaid cat sculptures. Cheap statuettes of Santeria Orishas and love potions were what they wanted.

"I've got an alibi, anyway," Furman said.

"Oh, you do?"

"He was killed Tuesday in the afternoon, right?"

"That's when the fire was. I don't know if the police determined the actual time of death."

"Well, I was here all day on Tuesday. I've got security-cameras in the store to prove it. In the morning, I came here straight from home, and the cops can check the cell towers pinged by my phone if they want."

The door to the street opened, and a customer entered. No, it wasn't a customer. It was Leticia, the restaurant owner I had spoken to previously. She was taken aback to see me here.

"Sorry," she said. "I didn't mean to interrupt."

"You're not interrupting," Fred said. "Ms. Mindle was about to leave."

"Hi, Leticia," I said.

"You two know each other?" Fred asked.

"I visited her establishment earlier."

"Ah, you're really doing the amateur-sleuth thing."

"I'm just a concerned citizen."

"I only came by to let you know it will be at ten tonight," Leticia said to Fred.

He nodded. I headed past her to the door.

"Thanks to both of you for speaking with me," I said.

Leticia made a serious mistake by letting me know an event of some sort was planned for tonight. I guessed she visited in person because she didn't want to call or text Fred in case her phone was subpoenaed.

In any case, I was determined to snoop on them.

On my way out, I brushed against the display case and grabbed Fred's white hairs that had fallen there.

We witches need our magic ingredients.

CHAPTER 7
HAIR OF THE WOLF

I brought Matt with me to stake out Fred Furman. I needed an accomplice for my safety when my consciousness was deep inside my penetration spell or if Furman found out he was being followed and attacked me.

We sat in my car across the street from Furman's boutique until he closed at 7:00 p.m. Then, we followed his car as he drove to my neighborhood and pulled into his driveway. We parked two houses down, where he wouldn't notice us, but we would see him when he pulled out. We planned to follow him to wherever the meeting would be.

"So," Matt said in the passenger seat, slapping his thighs.

"So, he's probably having dinner before heading to the merchant meeting."

"No, I meant a different kind of 'so.' Like, 'so, is this a good time to talk about us?' kind of 'so.'"

"Why would this be a good time for that?" I asked in all sincerity. "We're on a stakeout."

"Because we're sitting in your car with nothing to do, killing time until this guy leaves for the meeting. Rather than making silly small talk, we could discuss our relationship."

"Seems like an odd thing to talk about when we're tailing a werewolf."

"Missy, we're always following, or being chased by, supernatural creatures. That's normal for us."

"Yeah. It's part of our relationship."

"That's not the part I wanted to talk about."

"So, go ahead and talk about what you want to talk about."

"Have you had any change of feelings when it comes to us?"

"What do you mean?"

"You know what I mean," he said, losing patience. "Have I entrenched myself deeper into your heart?"

"You describe it like you're some sort of flesh-eating parasite. Which very well might be the next monster I'm assigned to document."

He sighed. "Are you feeling more romantic toward me?"

"Well, I grow ever fonder of you."

"I guess your answer is no, then."

"I didn't say that! Like I've told you, I was in a marriage that didn't work out. I'm not ready to be hurt again."

"I would never hurt you!"

"There's always a risk of being hurt in every romantic relationship. It will take me longer to be ready to dive in again than it would for someone who was never married."

"Like me?"

"Before I was married, I felt like I had a stopwatch timing how long it would take me to get hitched. It wasn't just my biological clock. It's the judgment of society, too. But now that

I've crossed it off my to-do list, I'm in absolutely no hurry to get married again."

"Are you implying I am?"

"You once said your mother didn't want to go to her grave without you being married."

"True. But I'm not in a hurry to satisfy her. I'm in love with you. It's that simple. I want to be in a loving relationship with you."

He had me cornered. I needed to be careful not to hurt him.

"I love you, too, Matt."

"But not in the same way?"

"As you surely remember, I told you I'm willing to take things in a physical direction. What I'm not yet willing to do is remember to buy anniversary presents, feel guilty when I want to be alone, constantly have to read someone else's mood, and respond to it. Etcetera, etcetera."

"You sound like a guy. Don't you want to have kids someday?"

"At my age, it's getting dangerously late for that. Besides, in my line of work, it would be irresponsible to bring a child into my life. I already have a mother threatening to kill my pets and enemies breaking into my house."

"I understand."

"Thank you."

"So," he said, slapping his thighs again.

"What kind of 'so' was that?"

"So . . . maybe I should stop demanding everything all at once. Maybe I should accept what you're willing to give now."

"Meaning?"

"Take things more physical. It could change your mind."

"It could also change yours. For the worse."

"No way."

"I hope you're not proposing getting it on right now in my car while we're staking out a werewolf."

"No. I'm proposing this."

He leaned over and kissed me on the lips. He was gentle and not intrusive, but he put a lot of feeling into it. I returned the feeling.

Hm, I thought. After a while, this *could* change my mind.

And in this manner, we killed the time before Fred Furman left his home. In fact, we killed it so delightfully that it went by quickly enough that we almost missed the taillights of Fred's car backing out of his driveway.

I pulled myself reluctantly from Matt's embrace.

"Time to play amateur sleuths again," I said, out of breath.

"I'm no amateur."

"No, you most certainly are not."

I FOLLOWED Furman at a safe distance, assuming he was returning downtown. But after heading north toward Jellyfish Beach Boulevard, he turned left before reaching it and remained on residential streets.

Up ahead was a small public park. The gate to the parking lot should have been locked at this hour, but it was wide open. Fred entered and parked among a dozen or so other cars.

I continued past the entrance and parked in front of a house just past the edge of the park.

"I really need to learn an invisibility spell," I said. "Though it wouldn't have been practical to use it at The Ripped Tide. The bar was too crowded, and people would have bumped into me. Plus, it would have been too difficult to slip into the storeroom with Maddie and Switchblade."

"What's wrong with the spell you used?"

"Nothing. It's just difficult and exhausting. Here, we're in an outside setting, and it's dark. If I were invisible, I could just wander into the park and observe."

"Furman's a werewolf. He would probably smell you."

"True. Well, let me get to work on the spell. I don't have to penetrate walls, but I have to connect with Fred over a distance."

I removed the Red Dragon talisman from its pouch and grasped it in my left hand while holding Furman's hair in my right. After conducting the spell-casting ritual, I used the psychic energy from the hair to locate its owner.

He was standing inside a pavilion beside an empty barbecue grill, illuminated by yellow lamps mounted on the ceiling. Before him were four picnic tables filled with men and women, most of whom I recognized as downtown business owners. My point-of-view was the same as Furman's, though more like from atop his head, as if the hair I held longed to return to its former home.

"Thank you all for coming here at such short notice," Furman said to the group. "And thanks to Leticia for coordinating a time when you all could fit it into your busy schedules."

"Speaking of busy, I need to get back to my pub," said a large, bearded guy who owned a high-end Irish establishment.

"You need your Guinness more than your pub needs you,

Damian," said an African American woman who owned an art gallery.

A few in the crowd laughed.

"I'll get right down to business," Furman said. "A detective spoke with me today about Dunott's death. It wasn't an accident. It was murder. Then, the same day, this crazy lady who owns a botanica was asking me about his murder."

Crazy lady? I tried not to let the insult affect my concentration and, thus, the spell.

"Who here has also been approached by someone asking about Dunott?"

They all raised their hands.

"Where have you been, Fred? This is old news," said Martha, the antique-store owner. "The police have been harassing us almost as much as Dunott was."

"I guess they don't see me as a suspect as much as they do you."

She barked a laugh. "Because my store is in the lower-rent area. And now, I hear talk that a few of my neighbors may have hired hitmen to take out Dunott."

This set the entire pavilion buzzing.

"Who?" Furman asked.

"Owners who aren't members of the Downtown Merchants Association. I won't say any names because it's just a rumor."

"Maddie Jong?" someone asked.

"What do you think?"

Several conversations began.

"Anyone else hear about hitmen?" Furman asked.

"What kind of coward would hire hitmen?" Damian asked angrily.

"We're all cowards," Furman said. "We let the abuse go on for so long, depending on the mayor and the city manager to help us, but they didn't. We begged the district attorney, the state attorney, and even the Feds to indict him, but nothing happened. The only blow we landed was the lawsuit, but that made Dunott abuse us more."

"Well, someone finally took care of it."

"You have something to confess, Damian?" asked the art-gallery owner.

Damian laughed bitterly. "I'm just saying you can be submissive for only so long before you can't take it anymore. We've always respected each other. Even you respect me, Cecily," he said to her, "though it doesn't seem like it."

Everyone laughed.

"Then Dunott comes along and crowns himself as the alpha of all of us."

"He was more powerful than we are," Martha said.

"Not all of us collectively," Damian replied.

"That's not how it works."

"Yeah, I guess not. We could have been stronger, but we just rolled over onto our backs and submitted to him. Until someone had to take it upon himself to end the dominance. All it took was a brave individual."

"Be careful what you say," Furman advised. "You don't want to implicate yourself."

"You think I did it? Well, I don't care!" Damian shouted. "Because I'm free again!"

He stood up from the picnic table. I tensed at the feeling he was going to do something dramatic.

And he did. He shifted into a wolf.

Right there, in front of the Downtown Merchants Association, his body contorted as his musculoskeletal system violently changed its shape and his clothing split apart. Fur sprouted rapidly as if I were watching stop-motion animation.

He groaned in pain. Until his groans turned into growls.

Not to be outdone, Furman shifted, too. I'd seen him in wolf form before, his white fur matching the color of his human hair. His wolf ears were no hairier than his human ones.

I didn't understand the logic of Furman shifting in front of everyone, unless it was a werewolf competitive thing he felt he had to do after Damian had shifted.

What happened next, I would not have expected in a million years. But it helped me understand the conversation right before this.

The entire group of Jellyfish Beach merchants shifted into wolves.

A good percentage of our local retailers and restauranteurs were werewolves. Can you say that about *your* town?

I've seen my share of werewolves shifting. It never gets easier to watch. The painful contortions make you feel sorry for the shifters, until you see how exhilarated they become once the transformation is complete.

Barks, yips, and howls punctuated the night. Nearby residents were surely calling in to report a pack of coyotes rampaging through the neighborhood.

In fact, from Furman's perspective, I saw movement near the far end of the park and frenzied barking.

It was a man walking his dog. If he approached any closer to the pavilion, he would see the group of werewolves his dog was barking at.

There was something about him that was familiar. I couldn't see his face clearly, but his tall, stooped posture was distinct.

It was time for Matt and me to get out of here before we were caught. I released the spell. Once I became reoriented to my body, I started up the car and floored it.

"What's wrong?" Matt asked.

"The Downtown Merchants Association just shifted into a pack of wolves."

"We have that many businesses run by werewolves? I thought most of the werewolves here were your former patients in Seaweed Manor."

"Apparently, Jellyfish Beach is Fur Town, USA."

I explained that this fact contributed to the conflict between the business community and Dunott.

"As a loup-garou, he was more powerful and deadly than they are. And he took advantage of that to be their alpha male."

"We keep discovering more motives for killing him," Matt said. "I'm surprised he wasn't murdered years ago."

"He only moved here from Canada a few years ago."

"I wonder why he moved here. Aside from the popular desire to move to warmer climes. Do you think it was because he knew we have a cornucopia of werewolves he could dominate?"

"Good question. We'll ask Furman. But not tonight. We'll confront him in his boutique when we know he won't shift and eat us."

"Yes, please. Confronting a cantankerous wolf is not a wise move."

"I'll admit," I said, "getting involved in solving this murder was not a wise move, either."

As we left the neighborhood, my memory kicked in. I remembered who the dog walker in the park reminded me of.

One of the goons belonging to the Knights Simplar. If it had really been that guy, and he had seen the werewolves, Jellyfish Beach was doomed to endure more violence.

Because the Knights Simplar had already learned that werewolves did, in fact, exist. And they wanted to kill them all.

CHAPTER 8
TRUTH SPELL

A mother, her two daughters, and their grandmother were in Furman's store when Matt and I stopped by. They were dressed expensively, and their manners oozed wealth. Perfect targets for Furman to unload overpriced, unnecessary cat novelties.

We waited patiently for Furman to sell them two fourteen-karat gold cat collars and a set of artisanal-catnip mice made by Tibetan monks. They turned down the cat paperweight he had tried to unload on me.

Finally, they left.

"You again?" Furman said to me. "Who's this guy?"

"I'm Matt Rosen." Matt didn't mention his job title, which was a good idea. He extended his hand, but Furman didn't shake it.

"I wanted to ask you a couple of additional questions," I said. "If you don't mind."

"Yes, I do mind. I've already told you everything I know

about Dunott. I don't have a clue who killed him. So, what else do you want from me?"

"The truth. You left out some pertinent details."

"Like what?" He pretended to busy himself refilling a self-service bin of catnip.

"We already knew that you're a werewolf. No big deal about that. But it would have been helpful to know that the entire Downtown Merchants Association is made up of werewolves."

He stiffened but didn't look at me.

"What gives you that idea?"

"I witnessed your meeting in the park last night."

"You were spying on us?"

"I was observing."

"You must have been using binoculars or some night-vision device, because we would have smelled you if you were at the park."

"Yes, I used special techniques."

"Witchcraft?"

"Yep."

"And just so you know, the association members are not all werewolves. We have several who are human and don't know about our true natures."

"Were they harassed by Dunott?"

"Not as much as we werewolves were."

"Are the owners of The Ripped Tide, Billy's Pizza, and the other businesses at that end of the boulevard werewolves, too?"

"The ones you mentioned are. But they're not members of the association. No loss, as far as I'm concerned."

"I met Maddie Jong and had no feeling at all that she was a werewolf," I said. "I can usually sense when someone is super-natural."

"Well, she is. And if you're interested in solving Dunott's murder, you should know that Maddie and a few others hired hitmen to do the job."

"We know about the hitmen," I said.

"You do? You were listening to us last night as well as watching us?"

"We already knew about the hitmen. Including the fact that they didn't do it."

"How do you know? They seem to me to be the most likely suspects."

"We spoke to the one who survived after Dunott attacked them."

Furman scratched his head. "You're a better amateur sleuth than I thought. But I suppose you depend upon your magic."

"Only when absolutely necessary." I admit I was peeved at his insinuation that my investigating didn't require cleverness on my part. "Tell me what it was like to be submissive to a loup-garou."

He frowned. "I don't like to be submissive to anyone. But we had no choice. Dunott was more powerful than we are. I'd never met a loup-garou before, and I thought they were only legendary figures. But he was even stronger and more savage than the legends."

"You guys couldn't have ganged up on him?" Matt asked.

"We tried once," Furman said angrily. "He killed two of us. Paul and Mark Levinson."

"The brothers that owned the Deli Twins restaurant?"

"Yeah."

"The police reported they had drowned in a fishing accident."

"No. Dunott tore them to pieces and threw them into the Intracoastal near the fishing pier at the causeway."

"Wow," Matt said. "The report said their bodies were damaged by sharks."

"No. By a loup-garou."

The three of us were silent for a moment, partly out of respect for the deceased, but I was also freaked out by the revelation.

"I was there," Furman said. "It wasn't even a contest. There were five of us from the association. It should have been a slam dunk, right? Five against one? It was a slaughter. The five of us shifted, but when Dunott shifted, he remained standing on two legs. I mean, he was a wolf in every way, covered in fur with a muzzle and terrifying canine teeth. But he stood on his hind legs, and his hands were like human hands."

"But still, five to one," Matt said.

"You know nothing. Dunott had an axe handle when we first confronted him. He had already told us he knew we were werewolves when he first visited each of us, demanding money. We didn't know what he was, but figured he was a werewolf, too, which was how he knew about us. I was surprised when I saw him with the axe handle. I thought maybe he wasn't a werewolf, or he wouldn't shift. Boy, was I wrong."

Furman closed his eyes as he relived the trauma.

"He shifted all right. But he still held onto the axe handle," Furman continued. "And he knew how to use it. He beat us to an inch of our lives."

"Werewolves have supernatural powers to heal from wounds," I said softly.

"We do. But broken bones take longer to heal. And Dunott was so fast and so strong that he broke a lot of bones that night. All of us were struggling to survive. Then Paul went down hard. Mark tried to save him, and Dunott beat him until the axe handle broke. Then. . ."

Furman struggled with his emotions.

"Then, while the rest of us were struggling to heal," he continued, "Dunott used his claws on the brothers. Even though he had human-like hands, his long nails were like razors. Finally, he opened his jaws—this bottomless pit of horror ringed with impossibly long teeth—and . . . we were forced to watch what he did to them so we would be too afraid to challenge him again."

"I'm sorry," I whispered.

"So, Dunott fancied himself the alpha of Jellyfish Beach after that. And no one had the courage to resist. I thought that's where the hitmen came in."

"Yes, they were hired," I said. "And they failed. Someone else must have found the courage."

"I don't know who."

"What about Damian? He sounded like he was up to the task."

"The magic you used to spy on us wasn't so good, because you missed the fact that Damian Connolly was full of his usual braggadocio."

I caught Matt's eyes and nodded.

"Is a loup-garou stronger than a normal human when in

human form?" Matt asked, distracting Furman like we had planned.

I took the opportunity to cast my truth-telling spell, discreetly sprinkling the powder onto Furman's feet while he leaned against the counter, looking in the opposite direction at Matt.

"They are said to be stronger," Furman replied. "None of us would try to fight him while we were in human form."

"So, if he were attacked while he was sleeping, and wasn't able to shift, he could be killed?"

"That's the premise," Furman said, his eyes already taking on the glassy, energized look that signified the spell was working.

"Someone like Damian in human form could shoot Dunott with regular bullets and kill him?" I asked.

"Yeah. But I don't think Damian did it," he replied in a strained voice that showed he was struggling to lie despite the spell.

"Tell me the truth. Do you suspect Damian?"

He sighed. "Yeah. He's the one I suspect the most. But I don't know for sure."

"You suspect him because of his bragging?"

"That and because Damian has a checkered past. There are stories he killed someone and got away with it before he moved here."

Furman had told me what I wanted to hear. But I hoped to get more before the spell wore off.

"If Damian didn't do it, who else would you suspect?"

"Come on, woman! Use your brain. Someone hired hitmen to do it. If you're right that the hitmen failed, whoever hired them would want to finish the job themselves or find another hitman."

"Who do you suspect, then?"

"Maddie Jong must be one of them. She's like the informal leader of the business owners on that end of the boulevard. And look at the place she runs! It's full of thugs and lowlifes."

"Not all of us are," Matt said.

I glared at him to shut up while I had Furman under the spell.

"Maddie only had to look across the bar to find criminals willing to kill someone," Furman said.

Before the spell wore off, I had one more question to ask.

"Did you kill Dunott, Fred? Tell me the truth."

"Me? Ha! Killing someone is not my style at all. I would have preferred to litigate him to death."

"Thank you," I said, breaking the spell. "Before we go, I'd like a few ounces of your freshest catnip."

It was too early for the lunch crowd at Finnegans Wake Pub. Only two men were at the bar sipping pints and watching a soccer match on TV. Damian Connolly sat hunched over a table by a window, working on a laptop and stroking his beard. Matt eyed the beer taps thirstily, but I gave him a small push to keep him moving with me toward Damian.

"Good morning," I said to him with a big smile. "I'm Missy and this is Matt. Do you mind if we ask you a few questions?"

"Regarding what?" His voice was hoarse, probably from his shouting, and then howling, last night. He looked much more relaxed now than he had at the park. His puffy face was no longer red, though his broad nose was. He smiled back at me, while his blue eyes studied us suspiciously beneath the bill of his trucker cap.

"We're working on an article for *The Jellyfish Beach Journal*," Matt said. "About the murder of Commissioner Dunott."

"I've got nothing to tell you. I barely knew him." Damian had a hint of an Irish brogue that I hadn't noticed before.

"We know he was harassing and extorting the downtown business owners, so obviously he had many enemies," I said. "We were wondering if you had any theories about who murdered him."

I attempted to cast my truth-telling spell.

"Why would you care what a humble pub owner like me would think?" He stood up from the table and walked toward the bar before I could sprinkle the powder on his feet. "Can I offer you two anything to drink?"

Matt and I scrambled after him.

"I'd love a bit of stout," Matt said, "though it's a bit early for me."

"It's never too early for a hearty drink. I think of stout as a meal."

Just as we reached the bar, Damian stepped back.

"Unfortunately," he said, "it looks like the keg needs changing. I'll have it ready in just a moment. You can keep talking."

He went through a doorway behind the bar.

"You're right that Dunott had a lot of enemies," Damian said, out of view. "Some of us have been more vocal than others in voicing our hatred of him."

I had the sudden fear that Damian was shifting back there

so he could return and eat us. Instead, he rolled a keg through the door and placed it in a fridge below the bar where he worked on hooking it up.

"Who would those people be?" Matt asked.

I moved opposite of where Damian was crouching behind the bar. Unfortunately, the two men at the end were watching me, so I couldn't sprinkle the powder on Damian's head.

"Fred Furman," Damian replied. "He's the president of the Downtown Merchants Association. I never thought he had it in him to break into someone's home, kill him, and set the place on fire. But people surprise you."

His head popped up above the bar, then he moved away from us to the taps. He opened the stout tap and ran the foam out.

"On the other hand, I've heard rumors that Maddie Jong of The Ripped Tide might've hired hitmen. Wouldn't be hard for her to do when you consider the clientele she serves."

"There are actually some very fine people who go there," Matt said.

Damian chuckled. "Yeah, right. Those who have paid their debts to society in prison, maybe."

I moved down the bar until I was across from Damian while he poured a pint. There was no way I could get my hand over the bar to sprinkle powder on him without him seeing what I was doing. I wished we had a table between us instead, where I could do the act beneath it.

"We've heard rumors that the hitmen messed up and didn't succeed," Matt said. He couldn't mention anything about a loup-garou in front of the other customers. Also, I didn't know if it would go well with Damian if we told him we knew he was a werewolf.

"I guess they hired idiots for the job. Never trust to someone else what you had better do yourself, I always say."

"What do you mean by that?"

"That Maddie should have done the job herself. Maybe she did."

He handed a pint of the dark brew to Matt, who appeared delighted to receive it.

"Shall we go back to your table to continue talking?" I asked.

Two couples walked into the pub.

"Morning! Sit wherever you like," Damian called to them. He turned back to us. "Sorry, I need to tend to them. My help won't be here for another half hour."

He went around the bar, carrying menus to the table the new arrivals had selected.

"We'll have to talk to him another time," I said to Matt.

We thanked Damian as we left and wished him a good day. I hadn't been able to use my spell on him, but my suspicions of him had increased.

CHAPTER 9
PROWLER

It was a rare, peaceful evening in the Mindle household. Mrs. Lupis and Mr. Lopez did not appear uninvited at my front door. Nor did police officers, Knights Simplar, vampires, solicitors, or religious evangelists.

My phone didn't ring all night. It would have been nice if Matt called just to say hello, but I nevertheless enjoyed the peace and quiet.

I made myself dinner featuring a sautéed filet of fresh vermillion snapper from the local fish market. It was followed by a leisurely bath. Then, I settled in on the sofa to read a new mystery novel. It was rather nice to experience crime-solving that I didn't have to do myself.

Witchcraft? Nope. No studying new spells or concocting potions. Tonight, I was simply a normal, divorced, forty-something woman in her cozy home.

Until Tony, my iguana witch's familiar, ruined the mood.

"Yo, something's out there," he said ominously in his New York accent.

I removed my eyes from my book to find the lizard on the coffee table looking at me.

"I beg your pardon?"

"There's an unfamiliar creature outside," he said. "Just out of range of the protective wards you put in the yard."

"You're like a trusty guard dog."

"I won't take that as an insult, since I was a dog in a previous incarnation. But I'm not sniffing or hearing this creature. I'm getting pinged by my sixth sense."

Bubba and Brenda, my tabbies, sat on the windowsill behind the curtains, staring outside. Their tails were twitching. My cats wouldn't qualify as guard cats, because while they demonstrated they had heard something outside, if that something tried to get into the house, they would instantly flee under the bed.

"I don't sense anything," I said. Having been born with the magic gene that foretold my destiny as a witch, I was more sensitive to supernatural activity than normal humans. I would usually know when something was nearby, be it a ghost or monster. But not tonight. And not as well as Tony, nor, apparently, my cats.

"You're too wrapped up in being a normal human tonight," Tony replied. "You've shut off your witchy self. Open your senses."

So much for my introspective evening off.

I put down my book, cleared my mind of trivial matters, and concentrated on my five normal senses plus my sixth. After a minute or so, a chill went down my spine and goosebumps covered my arms.

"Yes. I sense it. A powerful creature. Malevolent, too. Is it watching us?"

"Well, it hasn't moved, so it's not out there hunting or just passing by. Maybe there's nothing to be alarmed about, but we can't let down our guard."

I tried to return to my book, but I couldn't lose myself in it knowing a threat was nearby. Plus, I had an iguana staring at me from the coffee table.

"Do you mind giving me some space?" I asked as nicely as I could.

"Suit yourself." Tony's tiny claws clicked across the hardwood floors as he wandered into the kitchen instead of out to the garage where he belonged.

Again, I tried to read, but couldn't concentrate. My consciousness was too busy monitoring my property and its surroundings.

The cats' tails twitched more vigorously. Something was afoot.

I jumped as a whining sound filled my head. One of my wards had been triggered.

Tony raced into the living room. Iguanas can run faster than you'd think, so he was practically a blur.

"Fire up a protection spell," he said with rare fear in his voice.

I hadn't done so earlier, because my protection spells require a great deal of energy to cast and maintain. The threat had been uncertain. Not anymore. There was no time to use a magic circle like I normally would, but I was so familiar with this spell that I could cast it on the fly.

I enclosed the entire house in the spell's protective bubble. The larger the area I covered, the less-fortified any given spot of the bubble would be. This spell would probably not keep out a bullet, but no corporeal being could break through it, nor could most magical forces.

We were safe, but not relaxed. At all.

I turned off the lights inside and peered out the window. I saw nothing moving within the radius of the front-porch light that extended across my lawn into the edge of the street.

But I felt the presence strongly. Whatever type of creature it may be, it was evil.

Were there two yellow eyes glowing among the fronds of that areca palm tree?

"Werewolf," Tony said. "I think it's a male, though I can't say for sure."

"What does he want?"

"How am I supposed to know? I'm telepathic with you because I'm your familiar. I can't read the minds of random werewolves."

"He's not random when he's in my yard."

"Our yard."

"I pay the mortgage," I said. "My name is on the deed. This is my home."

"I'm not a pet."

"You're part of the family. This is your home, too. But I'm the head of the household. And why are we talking about this when there's a werewolf in *my* yard?"

"You're the one who veered off topic."

"Because I'm frightened."

The yellow eyes disappeared from the palm fronds. But before I could relax, another ward went off, its alarm filling my head.

"He set off another ward," I said. "I think he's really close, like beneath the window."

Tony and I jumped backward, away from the window. The cats had already disappeared from the sill and were most likely under my bed.

"It has to be Damian, stalking me because he knew we were on to him," I said. I had already told Tony about him.

Shh. He can probably hear you, Tony said telepathically.

How can I make him go away? I asked voicelessly.

You're the nurse for werewolves. Why are you asking me?

My portfolio of spells didn't include many offensive weapons. Attack spells were what black magic was about. My magic could only bother him with painful noise or unpleasant odors. But werewolves rarely abandon their prey.

Unless something else distracts them.

I conjured up a simple illusion, sending a small shadow racing across my lawn, followed by the scent of a rabbit. I hoped the wolf instinct would send the intruder after the fake rabbit.

It didn't. The glowing yellow eyes appeared just outside my window.

I stifled a shriek. The protection bubble vibrated as the creature flung himself against it. Just in case, I pumped more energy into the spell to strengthen it.

Would this go on all night? I feared I didn't have the strength to maintain the spell until dawn.

The eyes disappeared again, but I sensed the werewolf was still nearby.

Damian knew that I suspected he was Dunott's murderer. And he wanted to kill me, too.

What could I do except wait him out? I couldn't call the police, because the unwritten rule was that we of the supernatural world were forbidden to alert the police about our world. Nor could I call Matt because it would distract me from maintaining the protection spell. And he'd be foolhardy enough to drive over here to protect me and end up getting killed.

Just chill out, Tony said in my head. *He'll soon realize, if he hasn't already, that he can't get through the barrier. Eventually, he'll have to leave.*

Yeah, right. Like, I can really chill out.

But we waited, my iguana and I, crouched on the living room floor. About twenty minutes later, the wards' alarms fell silent. I sensed the creature had gone.

"He's out of here," Tony said aloud.

"Can you tell if he's still in the neighborhood?"

"It doesn't feel like he is. Better keep your protection spell up, just in case."

I didn't need him to tell me that.

"Be very careful," I said to Matt when he answered the phone. "A werewolf was stalking my home, and I think it was Damian."

"Did he leave?"

"Yes, but he might come after you next. You should come over here. I have the house under a protection spell."

"You mean like a slumber party?"

"No. I mean like a not-getting-eaten-by-a-werewolf party.

He came right up to the house, but the spell kept him out, and he left. All you have are locked doors, and those won't stop him."

"I'll be right there."

As I'd mentioned, the protection spell needed to be monitored and occasionally fortified. But if I pumped it full of magic juice, it would last long enough for Matt and me to sleep safely. I trusted the spell so much that I kept it going until Matt arrived, just in case the werewolf returned in the meantime.

When his truck pulled up, I called him and told him to wait until I released the spell, like disarming an alarm, so he could enter.

"Okay," I said. "The spell is turned off and I'm completely vulnerable."

As soon as Matt entered my home, I rebuilt the protection spell, and we were both encased inside.

I offered Matt a beer, though it was late enough that I needed to go to sleep. Since I never drank beer, I kept it in the garage fridge, where I also stored fresh ingredients for potions, like eyes of newt and the like.

When I entered the garage, Tony was on his wooden perch, trying to sleep.

"I see you have company. If you and pencil-neck are going to do the horizontal dance, can you please keep it down?"

"Get your mind out of the gutter, lizard."

I grabbed a few beers and turned off the garage light.

Matt sipped from a beer bottle while I recounted the werewolf encounter.

"How can you be so sure it was Damian?" he asked.

"Well, it could've been any of the werewolves in town, of

which we have way more than I had imagined. But I can't think of any werewolf who would be more likely to be alarmed by our questioning. I mean, at the meeting in the park, he practically admitted to killing Dunott. If he thought we suspected him, why not get rid of us?"

"Yeah. You're certain your protection spell is up and working?"

"Yes. We're safe in here."

"Could the werewolf have been Fred Furman? He lives so nearby."

"It wasn't him. I've seen him in wolf form before, and his eyes don't glow yellow like these."

"We should speak with him in the morning and ask him to keep his fellow werewolves on a short leash," Matt said, stifling a yawn.

"It's late," I said.

"I'll just crash here on the couch."

"Absolutely not. You'll be in the guest bedroom. There's an extra toothbrush in the guest bathroom."

"I brought my own."

"My, aren't you well prepared?" I stood and gave him a motherly kiss on the forehead. "See you in the morning."

Of course, I had the memory of our kissing in the car hanging over my head. But having your life in danger was the opposite of an aphrodisiac. So was being exhausted.

However, I woke up at 2:30 a.m. after a dream that I couldn't quite remember, yet it left me feeling frisky. I thought I should check on Matt and make sure he was in the guest bedroom and not on the couch.

I opened my door and tiptoed into the hall, wearing my

decidedly non-sexy pajamas. Glancing toward the living room, I saw the couch was empty. The heavy breathing of deep sleep came from the guest bedroom in front of me, through a door that hadn't been fully closed. Who knows why, but I peeked through the opening and saw Matt under the covers, bathed in the moonlight coming through blinds he hadn't closed.

I had the sudden urge to crawl into his bed without awakening him. Just sleeping beside him, perfectly innocent, sharing body warmth. That's all.

My feet moved of their own accord, and I drifted into the guest bedroom as if I were sleepwalking. I reached the empty side of the bed, lifted the covers, and—

Matt's phone dinged and vibrated. He clumsily reached for the phone, and the screen lit up his face.

"Wow," he muttered as he read his text. Then he noticed me standing there. "Hi. Fancy meeting you here."

"I was just checking on you."

"How kind of you. That text was from my editor. I need to go to a murder scene."

"Murder?"

"Yes. He heard on the police scanner that Damian's body was found behind Finnegans."

"Oh my," I said.

"Yes. Oh my, indeed."

CHAPTER 10
HUMAN OR ANIMAL?

By the time Matt and I arrived in the parking lot behind the pub, it seemed like half of the Jellyfish Beach Police Department was there, including both detectives, Shortle and Glasbag. Experiencing two murders in a matter of days was a big deal in our town.

Harsh light from streetlights reflected off asphalt slick from a light rain. The parking lot was empty except for the police cars and officers on its periphery, crime-scene techs, and three tarps covering the remains.

"There were *three* victims?" I asked Shortle.

"Nope. Just one," she replied. "Looks like one or more wild animals did the job."

"Oh." I shuddered at the implications. One or more werewolves had to have been responsible.

"You know anything about this?"

"No. Why would I?" I asked, feigning indignation.

"Because I chatted with Fred Furman yesterday, and he said

you two have been questioning our local merchants about Commissioner Dunott. You're basically duplicating the work I'm doing. Why would you do that?"

"I'm a reporter," Matt said. "The less information you provide to me, the more questions I have to ask."

"Why is she tagging along?" Shortle nodded at me.

"She's helping me."

It was the opposite of the dynamic of this investigation, but I kept my mouth shut. I couldn't explain the real reason I was probing the murder.

"It looks like Damian Connolly's death might be related to Dunott's," I said.

"Why would you say that?" Shortle asked.

"Damian was a loud opponent of his and his shakedowns."

"Yeah, but it looks like coyotes or something did this."

I'd hoped she would reveal something useful about Damian, but no such luck. I also resisted the temptation to point out that coyotes rarely attack humans and even more rarely kill them.

"When was the last time anyone saw Mr. Connolly?" Matt asked.

"How should I know? We got here only thirty minutes ago, and there were no witnesses, only the victim."

"Who reported finding the body?"

"Officer Jenkins." She pointed to a uniformed officer standing next to a patrol car at the edge of the parking lot. "He was doing a routine patrol of downtown when he found it."

"Can I speak to him?"

"I can't stop you."

Matt and I walked over to Officer Jenkins, a callow youth who still had acne. He looked sick to his stomach.

Matt introduced us and flashed his press badge.

"Did you just come upon the body, or did anything lure you into this parking lot?" Matt asked.

"I always patrol back here. Burglars like to break in through the back doors of the businesses. And sometimes, I'll find a stolen car parked in rear parking lots like this where it's hidden from traffic on the boulevard."

"Did you see a suspect or anyone else?"

"No. I mean, I thought I got a glimpse of someone running away, but it had to have been an animal. A dog or coyote."

"Just one?"

"Yeah. And like I said, I'm not even sure I saw it."

"Was it a person or an animal?" I asked.

"It had to be an animal. I mean, it seemed tall, but I thought I saw fur."

"It sounds like you really didn't see it well."

"It was probably just a shadow. Or a coyote. The medical examiner has to figure out if the victim was killed first before the animals got to him."

"So, a human could have killed him, then the animals set upon the corpse?" Matt asked.

The officer nodded.

"You're saying you could have seen the human, or an animal, or both?"

"I'm not sure. It was a shadow in the alley over there. It moved so fast."

It sounded to me like the officer had seen the werewolf. It might have been in the process of shifting back to human form when he saw it. As a member of the Friends of Cryptids Society, I had the duty to prevent knowledge of the supernatural spreading among normal humans. This required action.

I clutched the power charm that was always in my pocket and cast a simple spell on the officer. It would cloud his memory so no retrospection or therapy would reveal the true image of what he'd seen. I felt guilty about invading the brain of someone who wasn't a criminal, but it was for the greater good.

Matt looked at me. He knew I was casting a spell and probably knew why. He nodded his approval.

A white SUV belonging to the medical examiner arrived. The woman, in her early sixties, got out and spoke to the detectives before approaching the victim's remains. Before she pulled back the tarps, Shortle asked us politely to leave the scene. I was all too happy to obey.

"With Damian dead, does this mean we don't have to worry about the werewolf who was stalking you?" Matt asked after we got into the cab of his truck.

"I hope so. I wonder why he was killed. Another werewolf obviously did it."

"The other werewolves knew he was a hothead who could reveal their secrets. And if he really was the one who murdered Dunott, he'd be a huge liability for them. So they got rid of him."

"Sounds plausible," I said.

"Since he won't be lurking outside of your house, I'll drop you off and get out of your hair."

"Maybe you'd better stay just in case," I replied. And I was speaking only out of an abundance of caution. Really. "Because what if the werewolf that was stalking me wasn't Damian? That would mean he or she is still out there."

"If that's the case, do we assume it was the same werewolf who killed Damian?"

"I don't know."

"If so, it probably had its fill of killing for the time being."

"Would you bet your life on it?"

Matt chuckled. "No. You're right. We'll spend the rest of the night under your protection spell."

"And in the morning, we'll pay a visit to Fred Furman. If he's not in a cranky mood, he might shed some light on this. But don't bet on him not being cranky."

When we returned to my house, I checked on the wards, then cast another protection spell. It was nearly 4:00 a.m., and I was too tired to sneak into Matt's bed.

That's what happens when you're my age.

"No, I hadn't heard about it," Fred Furman said, appearing sincere. "My garsh, that's horrible. Poor Damian."

"It happened early this morning, too early to make the newspaper," I said, "but they mentioned it on the TV news."

"I get all my news from social media. I'm not so good at what's happening in the world, but I know all the best conspiracy theories."

"The body was mauled like a wolf attack. Do you think any members of the Downtown Merchants Association were responsible?"

"I don't know. I can't think of a reason anyone would want to kill Damian."

"Because he sounded guilty of Dunott's murder. Maybe someone was afraid he'd bring police scrutiny to the business owners and reveal the existence of werewolves."

"Killing Damian the way you said he was killed will bring the same scrutiny."

"True," I admitted. "I'm just grasping at theories."

"Why don't you let the police do their jobs?"

"They're not very good at their jobs here in Jellyfish Beach," Matt said. "And as a journalist, I refuse to accept only what facts they decide to give me. We're investigating because the public deserves to know the truth."

Actually, I thought, it's quite the opposite. We want to know the truth, but we don't want to let the public know any part of it that involves the supernatural.

"Did you ask nosy questions of Damian like you did with me?" Furman asked.

"Yes," I said.

"Someone could be sending a message to the other business owners not to talk to you guys."

"Why?"

"Well, did Damian have a theory of who murdered Dunott?"

"He thought Maddie Jong could have done it."

"Of course, she could have done it!" Furman said. "She hired the hitmen, after all."

"We told you the hitmen didn't do it."

"Maddie must have finished the job."

"When Dunott was killed, she thought the hitmen did it."

"How do you know that?"

"Um, we can't say."

"You were spying on her, like you did me and the association."

"Something like that."

"She was probably misleading you. Consensus has been building along the boulevard that she murdered Dunott," Furman said. "And Damian was the loudest about it. I, too, bet she killed him."

Matt and I exchanged glances. I think we both agreed with Furman.

I studied the old shifter, looking for signs of lying. There weren't any, of course. He was only repeating what he'd told us under the truth spell.

"Fred, I have one more question for you. Were you stalking my house in wolf form last night?"

"No. Why would I do that?"

"Do your eyes glow yellow when you're a wolf?"

"I rarely admire myself in the mirror when I shift," he replied. "But no, they don't."

"A supernatural creature was lurking outside my home. I'm pretty sure it was a werewolf. I had thought it was Damian, but he was murdered behind his bar, possibly around the same time."

"It could have been him, depending upon the time of death. He could have gone to his pub after leaving your home. Then again, maybe it was Maddie."

I sighed. No matter how law-abiding they are in human form, werewolves tend to kill other creatures. It's in their nature. And when you have an entire business district filled with them, it leaves you with too many suspects.

We thanked Fred and left his boutique.

"We need to talk to Maddie," I said.

"I'm not so sure that will do any good."

"It can't hurt to try. I'll use my truth spell."

"To be honest, it makes me uncomfortable trying to incriminate Maddie," Matt said as he climbed into his truck. "I'm a regular at her bar. She's like family to me."

"You said she punched you in the jaw."

"That was perfectly understandable. I had asked her if she rode a Japanese motorcycle."

I rolled my eyes. "I'll pick you up after work, and we'll go to The Ripped Tide."

"I'll never be able to drink there again." Matt pouted.

WE SAT in my car in The Ripped Tide's parking lot beside the railroad tracks. The country music blaring from an open back door made my steering wheel vibrate. I admit that I wasn't sure of the best way to proceed. Maddie wasn't the type who would easily agree to a quiet sit-down meeting with us where I could use my truth spell.

But just then, Shortle walked around from the front of the bar, got into her unmarked Ford parked close to the building, and drove away. She didn't notice us in our shadowed parking spot.

"Shortle must have been talking to Maddie," I said. "This might give us an opportunity, like with the bump sting, to eavesdrop on her if Shortle was aggressive enough to rattle her."

I reached into the back seat and grabbed my tote bag. The sandwich baggie in which I had placed Maddie's hair was still there. The hair had little of her psychic energy remaining. It would be challenging to repeat the spell I had used to learn about the hitmen.

While I prepared the spell, a car arrived in the parking lot. Boris Jones got out and went into the bar. He owned a convenience store on the other side of the tracks on an even lower-rent stretch of the boulevard than where we were. I wondered if he was in cahoots with Maddie.

Matt remained quiet while I gathered my energies and mouthed the words to the incantation. My consciousness detached itself from my body. The spell was working. Soon, I was in the storage room that Maddie used as an office. I looked down upon her sitting in a chair swiveled away from her desk and facing Johnny of Billy's Pizza and Boris.

"You heard that Damian was murdered?" she asked.

The two men nodded.

"Do you think werewolves did it?" Johnny asked.

"Yeah," Maddie replied. "Or something more powerful."

"Like what?"

"A loup-garou. There have been whisperings among our community that another one is in town."

"Maybe it knew Dunott," Boris said.

"Maybe it killed him."

"The way Dunott died, it doesn't seem like a loup-garou did it," Johnny said.

Maddie shrugged. "Thing is, Detective Shortle seems to

think I did it. She was here just now, asking me questions about Damian. That's why I wanted to talk to you guys. But she also asked me a lot of questions about Dunott."

"Ya know, I was thinking Damian killed him."

"Me, too," Maddie said.

"What the heck is that?" Matt asked at the periphery of my consciousness. I ignored him so my spell wouldn't break.

I kind of wished I hadn't.

Because, with a loud boom, the storeroom's door blew open. Maddie and the others looked up in horror.

A giant man walked into the room. Only, he wasn't really a man. He was covered in a coat of thick black fur, sleek and shiny. At the ends of his hairy fingers were long, needle-like nails.

And his head was that of a wolf, with eyes that glowed yellow.

I recognized those eyes from the darkness outside my house the previous night.

The creature was a loup-garou.

CHAPTER II

LOUP-GAROU TIMES TWO

oris was sitting closest to the door. He jumped up from his chair, and a backhand from the loup-garou sent him flying into the shelves of liquor. A bottle of bourbon fell to the floor and shattered. This penetration spell was so effective I could smell the spilled booze.

The slight delay to get Boris out of his path slowed the beast just enough to allow Maddie and Johnny to comprehend what they were up against.

They both shifted into wolves.

But it was obvious the loup-garou had one specific target: Maddie. He lunged at her, raking her with his claws while she was struggling to complete her shifting.

Johnny was not finished either, though he still tried to shield Maddie with his body. As wolves, they had better odds against the creature, but their vulnerability during their transformations might be their undoing.

The monster flung Johnny across the room, then stood over

Maddie as she tried to finish shifting and heal herself of the claw wounds at the same time.

I couldn't do anything to help Maddie and the others while I was locked in this spell. It took so much of my energy, I didn't have enough to cast my sleep and immobility spells on the loup-garou at the same time. Ironically, if I released the spell, I'd lose the visual of the office—and the targets—and wouldn't be able to use those spells anyway.

I needed to go inside. Into the meat grinder. Fear made me hesitate.

Meanwhile, Boris got to his feet amid the broken glass. He didn't shift. He simply pulled a gun from his waistband and fired at their attacker.

A werewolf can't use silver bullets, so the standard ammo couldn't kill the loup-garou. It could distract him, though, and cause bar goers to call the police.

Maddie and Johnny were fully wolves now, but they still wouldn't survive long against a loup-garou.

The monster staggered backward from the gunshots. And then he leaped at Boris, slashing him with deadly claws.

Maddie and Johnny sank their long canine teeth into the bipedal loup-garou's legs, but he kicked and flung them off like they were small terriers.

Distraction was the only way I'd get inside and survive. I released the spell.

"Matt, call nine-one-one."

"I did as soon as I heard the gunfire."

I had noticed fire sprinklers on the ceiling of the storeroom. I cast a heat spell, making it strong enough to set off the sprinklers.

Then, I ran toward the back door of the building.

"Missy!" Matt shouted. "Stop! Don't be crazy!"

Patrons poured from the doorway. I pushed through them and got far enough inside to see the broken door of the storeroom.

I conjured a smoke bomb and set it off in the room.

As a nearby sprinkler soaked me, two wolves darted from the room and escaped the building.

The loup-garou and Boris were still in the room. I willed myself to move toward the door. Once I saw the loup-garou, I could immobilize him with my magic.

Assuming he didn't disembowel me immediately.

Smoke continued to pour from the room, past the splintered door hanging crookedly from a solitary, bent hinge. My hands shook, even my left that held my power charm.

Suddenly, a large humanoid figure ran from the room, obscured by the smoke. He was naked, with long, wet hair that covered his face. I saw him for only a second, too brief to cast a spell on him, before he disappeared from the building.

Someone was still in the storeroom. It was Boris. He lay crumpled in the corner beside the shelves. A quick look was all it took to tell me he was dead.

DETECTIVE SHORTLE WAS SATISFIED by the tale Matt and I told. We said we had just arrived in the parking lot when we heard shots fired inside. Matt said he called 911, as did other patrons, and we didn't see who had fired the shots.

I hovered nearby while Maddie, now in human form,

explained that there had been an altercation between Boris and an unknown party that had spilled over into the storeroom where Boris shot at the man, apparently missing him. Johnny backed up her story. The wounds they had sustained had healed while they were in wolf form.

Maddie asserted the stranger must have been armed with a cleaver or a similar weapon.

"That was a loup-garou, right?" I asked her after Shortle had stepped away.

She looked at me with surprise.

"I know all about them," I said. "And all about you were-wolves. You don't have to give me a cover story. The loup-garou killed Damian, I'm pretty sure about that. And he tried to kill you. Did he kill Dunott, too?"

After what I'd overheard through my spell, I was pretty sure Maddie was innocent of Dunott's murder.

"I don't know. He could've killed him. It could've been a territorial thing between loup-garous."

That seemed to me to be the most likely explanation. Nevertheless, I wasn't satisfied. I felt like there was more of a story out there in the darkness, beyond my vision.

And I want you to know that Jellyfish Beach is a safe town. Really. Despite a monster having killed three people. Could happen anywhere, right?

"WHAT A SURPRISE TO SEE YOU TWO," I said, opening the front door for my Society handlers only minutes after I had returned home.

They ignored my sarcasm.

"A second loup-garou has come to our area," Mrs. Lupis said excitedly.

"It sure has," I said. "I saw it."

"Please don't tell us you neglected to take a photo yet again," Mr. Lopez said with his own sarcasm.

I *had* neglected to do so. The only time I saw it was via my penetration spell, not counting my brief, fragmented view of the monster in human form.

Fortunately, trusty Matt had been fiddling with his phone in the car while I was conducting my spell. He managed to get a not-so-good shot of the beast before it entered The Ripped Tide, and he had sent it to me.

"It's not the best picture, but it's all we could get." I showed them my phone. "I'm pretty sure it's a male, though it's hard to tell with all his fur."

They nodded in unison.

"This matches other witness accounts," Mr. Lopez said.

"And the centuries-old legends," his partner added.

"I saw him in action, thanks to a spell I was using. Of course, I couldn't record what I was seeing magically. Come with me to the kitchen, and I'll tell you over some hot tea."

I recounted the fight at the bar and what had happened to Damian. My narration included everything else that had happened before tonight that my handlers hadn't heard about.

"Remarkable," Mr. Lopez said at my kitchen table.

"How did it escape our notice that there were so many werewolves among the business community?" Mrs. Lupis asked.

"We knew they were predators," I said, "but not the super-natural kind."

The two didn't laugh at my joke.

"It's also remarkable to have two loup-garous in the same city, let alone the same county," Mr. Lopez said. "Their need for territory is why so many migrated from the original French-speaking colonies."

"Is that why the second one killed Dunott?" I asked. "To take over his territory?"

"Oh, we don't think he murdered Dunott."

"Not based upon the facts you've given us," Mrs. Lupis added.

"Really?" I asked. "It seems like the most obvious conclusion." It also would mean I didn't have to struggle to solve the mystery anymore.

"Loup-garous only fight and kill another of their kind when in full monster form. It's a matter of pride and dominance display," Mr. Lopez explained. "They would never shoot their opponent, especially not in human form."

"Our theory is that the second loup-garou knew Dunott from before. That they were friends or relatives."

"Yes. And the second one came here to avenge Dunott's death."

"Oh my," I said.

"And you'll be amused by this," Mr. Lopez added. "Our theory is that the second loup-garou is tracking your progress with the investigation somehow, perhaps through telepathy or similar paranormal ability. He discovers who you suspect, then he kills them."

"Oh my." My stomach throbbed with pain. "But I was

wrong about Maddie being the murderer. And I haven't proved that Damian did it. He and Boris died because of me?"

"No, their deaths weren't your fault," Mrs. Lupis said with a hint of sympathy in her voice. I think that was the most emotion I've ever witnessed in her. "It was irresponsible for the loup-garou to act based on your speculation. He must have known you weren't certain about who you suspected. But killed them anyway."

"Loup-garous enjoy killing," said Mr. Lopez. "Any excuse is good enough for them."

"Thanks," I said, "but I'm not feeling any better. I think it's best if I stop investigating."

"Oh, no. You must continue," they said together.

"The Society is depending on you," Mrs. Lupis said.

"If not you, the monster would track whoever the police suspect," said Mr. Lopez. "They're more likely to make stupid assumptions than you are."

"Thank you. I guess."

"There is one possible solution to this quandary. Assuming the second loup-garou is here to exact revenge, perhaps you can convince him to be more patient and wait until you finally solve the mystery."

"You've got to be kidding."

"No," Mr. Lopez said. "I'm not. This is an intelligent creature, and he might agree to be more reasonable."

I put my face in my hands. It was times like this that I missed my nerve-wracking twelve-hour shifts in the intensive care unit.

"THEY THINK the loup-garou is following *us*?" Matt asked.

"Yes. And killing our suspects. I guess he's not much of a detective."

"Nor is he a judge. He's just the executioner."

"I guess monsters don't care much about justice. Just revenge."

"Well, if you have anyone you want to get rid of, let's pretend they're a suspect."

"I wouldn't wish a loup-garou attack on anyone," I said, even though my evil mother came to mind.

"Especially not us. I don't like the idea of him following us. Why was he trying to break into your home if he's just observing?"

"I don't know. Maybe he wasn't trying to break in and just wanted to be closer to read my mind. Maybe my imagination got the best of me."

"I'm afraid now to even think of who's guilty," Matt said.

"Shouldn't be a problem because I have no idea. We have to go back to square one. The local business owners still have the strongest motive to have killed Dunott, and a lot of them have probably thought about it."

"My money is on Furman, even though he claims to have an alibi. But I think we should have another chat with Mrs. Dunott to see if there are any clues she might have overlooked."

GEORGETTE WASN'T STAYING with her neighbor, having moved into a condo while her home was renovated to repair the fire damage. The neighbor was protecting Georgette from nosy people like us and wouldn't tell us where she was. I hadn't wanted to bother her for her phone number right after her husband's murder, even though Matt had wanted it.

I convinced the neighbor to call or text Georgette to ask her if it was okay if we paid a visit. She replied immediately that it was all right with her.

"Let's not bring up shifters or anything supernatural with her," I said to Matt on the way. "Let's make her as comfortable as possible. Asking about Dunott being a loup-garou will only make her defensive."

"Missy, I do this for a living."

"And I deal with the supernatural for a living."

The condo was in a small building on the beach, near the intersection of Jellyfish Beach Boulevard and A1A. I should add that it was an ultra-luxury condo with a stunning view of the ocean.

Her husband had allegedly been an attorney, though he wasn't associated with any law firm. I had a feeling the couple's extravagant lifestyle was paid for by his illegal revenues.

"I heard that two local business owners were murdered," she said as soon as we sat down in the living room. "Did they have anything to do with Pierre's murder?"

We were pretty certain the murders were related, but we pretended not to know.

"We agree with what you said before, that someone from the business community was responsible for your husband's murder," I said. "We're doing our best to investigate, but any suspicions you have would be helpful."

"I told you the owner of that nasty bar was very hostile."

"We don't believe she was responsible," Matt replied. Even though Maddie had organized a failed attempt.

"Well, I don't have any clues, if that's what you're asking for."

"Which business owners have you or Pierre interacted with most recently?" I asked.

"Let me think. Oh yes, the wall clock above the sofa. I bought it from that charming cat boutique." She pointed at a colorful blown-glass clock in the style of Chihuly, with a swinging pendulum shaped like a cat's tail. "The owner there, Fred Furman, was gruff but gracious."

"Anyone else?" Matt asked.

"The night before Pierre died, we had a lovely meal at that Argentinian place. The owner there is such a dear friend of Pierre's that she comped our meal. In fact, she did that every time we visited. We had a reservation for the upcoming week-end, but she abruptly cancelled it for no good reason."

She frowned, as if this had been a great insult. I noticed for the first time the lines around her brown eyes on her otherwise porcelain skin.

"Leticia Maldonado allowed you to eat at her restaurant for free?" Matt asked.

"Yes. She considered us friends and was delighted by the good work Pierre was doing on the commission."

This didn't sound like the restaurant owner we had spoken to.

"How generous," Matt said, unable to keep the sarcasm from his voice.

I recalled that Maddie had accused Dunott of having had extramarital affairs.

"How was your relationship with Pierre?" I asked.

"It was wonderful. We were best friends, closer than ever in his last days." She dabbed at her eyes with a tissue. The emotion seemed genuine, but who was I to judge?

I ruled out using a truth spell on her, at least not now. Not unless we suspected she was trying to protect the murderer.

"Was there anyone besides Maddie Jong who was openly hostile toward your husband?" Matt asked.

"When you're in politics, you'll always encounter hostility. But no, there's no one who stands out. Except for Fred, since he's the president of the Downtown Merchants Association. He butted heads with Pierre a lot, but Fred never threatened him or anything. And it didn't keep me from shopping at his boutique." She gave a nod to the Chihuly clock.

We were getting nowhere, so I took a different tack.

"Where did you and Pierre first meet?"

She smiled. "In Savannah. I had just graduated from art school, and Pierre moved there from Quebec City, where he had grown up. He went to law school in Louisiana, then moved to South Carolina, where he passed the bar exam. Five years ago, we moved to Jellyfish Beach, and Pierre passed the Florida bar."

"Why did you move to Florida?"

"Because of Jellyfish Beach. Such a wonderful, unique place. Pierre saw lots of opportunities here."

He saw a town filled with werewolves he could dominate and exploit, I thought.

"Did he practice law here?"

"At first, but then he got involved in politics. The city commission took up all his time."

I knew that city commissioner was only a part-time job. All

the other commissioners kept their day jobs. I guessed corruption was Dunott's day job.

"Did Pierre remain close to his friends and family in Canada?"

She cocked her head as if surprised by my question.

"He was quite close to his brother," she replied. "They were twins. Very, very close, even though Claude lives in Canada. In fact, when I called to tell Claude that Pierre had passed, Claude already knew. He said he'd had a feeling in his gut that day and just knew something had happened to Pierre. I guess it was that special connection that twins have."

"Oh my. Is Claude coming to Florida for the service?"

"Not for the main service this week. The family wants to have a second one in Quebec City. But I wouldn't be surprised if Claude visits Jellyfish Beach at some point. He would want to be sure that the murderer is caught, and justice is done. The Dunott family is unique when it comes to their . . . principles."

Evidence appeared to point to Claude already being in Jellyfish Beach, trying to find his own form of justice exacted with jaws and claws. The loup-garou principles.

It felt like we were no closer to finding Pierre's murderer while an entire rash of new murders were breaking out.

CHAPTER 12
COMMUNITY IMPROVEMENTS

"Good heavens! She looks delicious!" said the elderly vampire in a nun's habit. She stood just beyond the entrance as Agnes opened her door.

"Missy, this is my ancient friend, Mathilda," Agnes said before turning to her guest. "And you should know it's absolutely forbidden to feed on Missy."

"What a shame. Her blood smells delightful. Type O?" she asked me.

"Yes. And it's very precious to me."

"If you lose a little, your body will make more."

"Mathilda!" Agnes scolded. "You act like you've never been out of the convent before."

"I only go out to feed. My current convent is all vampires now."

"You need a blood-donation bus to bring your meals every night like we have."

"I know. That's so convenient. I've grown tired of hunting

prey. That's how I broke my tooth; my prey's pearl necklace got in the way."

"Speaking of which," I said, "I have a spell and a potion for you that should repair your tooth. Agnes asked me to create them for you."

"I'm sorry," Agnes said. "Come in, dear, and have a seat. Mathilda gets so excited, and it distracts me."

"That's the case with you youngsters," Mathilda said.

Agnes must have noticed the confused expression on my face. Though Mathilda was probably in her seventies in body age, Agnes was ninety.

"Having existed for fifteen hundred years makes me a baby compared to Mathilda," Agnes said. "She was turned over two thousand years ago."

"I was around when Christ himself walked the earth. Too bad I lived in what we now call Germany and never got to meet him. But since I took my vows, I feel I know him very well."

"Were you turned before or after you became a nun?" I asked.

"Before, you tasty little one. They didn't have Christianity in Germany until centuries later."

"How did you guys meet if Mathilda was isolated in a convent?"

"It wasn't easy to survive during the Dark Ages if you were ninety in body age," Agnes said. "Even if you were a vampire. I lived with the descendants of my human children until the constant warfare and the spread of Christianity made that impossible. I was on my own until I met Mathilda."

"Convents were very different back then," Mathilda said. "They were far from being hermetically sealed from the outside world. Many young women would live there, with or without taking vows, sent there because they were unmarried, and their families couldn't support them. We also took in refugees. Like Agnes."

"Yes, I was hunting for humans one night, close to starvation, when I ran into Mathilda. She took pity on me and invited me to her convent. I never took vows but lived there for centuries."

"But then, that Martin Luther fellow came along and made things difficult for the Catholic Church. A bunch of us moved to Vatican City."

"Rome was a wonderful place to spend the centuries," Agnes said. "Until the fascists took over in the 1920s. The same group of us moved to America, to New York City. The sisters founded a new convent upstate, but I stayed in the city. Finally, I moved down here to Florida. After hundreds and hundreds of years, I'd finally had enough of winter weather."

"It's nice that you two have stayed in touch," I said.

"Indeed," Mathilda said. "And this is my first time visiting Squid Tower. Such a lovely place, but I already have ideas of how you, as the nest mother, can improve things."

"That's my informal status," Agnes said. "Technically, I'm just the president of the homeowners' association."

"The title doesn't matter."

"Oh, yes, it does. The residents here can be very ornery."

"Are you ready for your spell now?" I asked, trying to get things back on track.

"I am," Mathilda said. "My tooth is terribly painful. I don't understand why my vampire healing powers don't work on it."

"Because you must have damaged the tooth before you

were turned. It was probably intact but weakened for centuries until the pearl necklace finally broke it. My spell and potion should take care of it, though. As a nun, do you have any issue with me using pagan magic on you?"

"Of course not! I'm a supernatural creature. I've had to bend quite a bit of doctrine to accommodate my nature."

I led Mathilda into Agnes's kitchen, where I drew a large magic circle on the floor with a dry-erase marker. We both knelt within it, facing each other. Try as I might, I couldn't shake the discomfort of having a predator only inches away from me.

Let's get this over with, I thought to myself, and began my usual ritual of gathering my internal energies and the elemental ones. Next, I pulled out my crib notes: the spell's incantation that Don Mateo had dictated to me.

In my other hand, I held a vial of the potion, which I had mixed in my garage workshop the previous night.

After I recited the spell, I sent energy into Mathilda's mouth and the vial. The glass burned in my hand, almost too hot to hold.

Mathilda's head jerked backward. Her eyes filled with surprise.

"Quick, take one sip of this." I handed her the vial. "And gargle with it before swallowing."

She removed the stopper and did as I asked, tilting her head back as she gargled. The sight of the fanged creature gargling was both hilarious and horrifying.

After she swallowed, she ran her tongue over the molar in question.

"Goodness gracious!" she exclaimed. "The crack in the tooth is gone!"

I pulled a hand mirror from my tote bag and handed it to her. She studied the inside of her mouth.

"Yes, it looks good as new!"

"Take one sip of the potion every night until it is gone. It will ensure that the tooth is strong again."

"Thank you so much. How can I repay you?"

I stood and stepped from the magic circle, releasing the spell. After I quit the home-nursing agency and saw a few patients on my own, I charged quite modest fees. But what would a nun be able to afford?

Before I could answer, she pushed a wad of cash into my hand.

"Oh, this is too much," I said, counting it.

"Nonsense. You provided a service I could not get elsewhere. And I am grateful."

It worried me to be overpaid by a vampire. I didn't want to be under any obligation to her. But on the other hand, I was spending way too much time investigating murders for free. It felt nice to profit for once.

"Now that my tooth is taken care of, let's go for a walk," Mathilda said to Agnes. "I want to point out some of the ideas I had for improving your community."

"Improve?"

"Having my vocation for over a millennium has taught me discipline and efficiency. I think my ideas will greatly benefit Squid Tower. Especially if I decide to move here."

"Move here?"

"Yes. I believe it's time to say goodbye to winter weather for good."

"Are you becoming a lay person?"

"No. I'll remain a nun. But I could never fit in at a human convent in this day and age. If things work out, I might move our vampire convent down here from New York. Shall we go for our walk now?"

"Yes," Agnes said warily. She gestured for me to accompany them. For moral support, I assumed.

During our elevator ride to the ground floor, Mathilda peered at the inspection certificate mounted beside the control panel.

"The elevator is way overdue for an inspection."

"Yes," Agnes replied. "Handling the inspectors is difficult for us, in that they only work during the day. We used to employ a human to deal with human contractors and officials. She didn't know we were vampires; we told her we were a leper colony. Unfortunately, she stayed here too late one night, and a resident fed on her, breaking the rules. She quit after that."

"Good help is hard to find," I said, thinking about the gate guard, Bernie, and how short his tenure on the overnight shift had been before he was turned.

"Don't you feel unsafe in an uninspected elevator?" Mathilda asked.

"If it dropped, we vampires could heal from our injuries," Agnes replied.

My heart froze. "Can you let me out on the next floor? I'll take the stairs."

"Don't be silly. Here we are on the ground floor now."

"Shall we walk past the community rooms?" Mathilda said.

"Of course." Agnes led us past the large multi-purpose room, a kitchen that was never used, a gym that was rarely used because the weight machines were too easy for vampires, and the card room.

"This room," Mathilda said in the card room, "can become a chapel."

"But our residents like to play cards and board games."

"I don't approve of card games. Bingo is fine, but that can be played in the large room."

"And it is," I said, though I avoided Bingo Night. Vampires are extra dangerous then.

"I think a chapel would be a better use of this room," Mathilda said.

"This is difficult to explain to you," Agnes said, hesitantly. "You took your vows so long ago. But as a general rule, vampires aren't super religious. Most supernatural monsters aren't. Some residents occasionally have informal services in the main room out of nostalgia for whatever religion they followed as humans. But a chapel wouldn't go over well with the residents."

"Sometimes, we don't know what's best for us until we're forced to accept it."

"No. We must vote on everything here. Trust me, these vampires don't want to be told what to do."

"We'll come back to this," Mathilda said, walking down the hall to the glass door that led to the pool deck. "Next, we should discuss a dress code."

Several female vampires were participating in a pool aerobics class while men and women lay on loungers around the pool, soaking in the moonlight. The women were all in one-piece bathing suits, and the men wore baggy trunks. There were no bikinis or thongs in sight.

"Showing flesh like that isn't just immodest," Mathilda said. "It's immoral."

It was also hard on the eyes with all those pasty complexions, I thought.

"Our residents prefer to live in the twenty-first century," Agnes replied. "Plenty of them were humans back when bathing suits covered your entire body, but they've adapted. And I disagree with you calling them immoral. As vampires, we're amoral."

Mathilda sighed with exasperation.

"You can take the nun out of the convent, but not the convent out of the nun," I said. I was trying to be funny, but the glares from the two vampires put a chill in my blood.

"There's more," Mathilda said. "I'm not finished yet."

We followed her around the building to the recreational area. We passed the shuffleboard and bocci courts. The horseshoe pit, which no one used. And the tennis courts that had been converted for pickleball. Aside from the horseshoe pit, every venue was packed with vampires.

"We're quite an active community for our body ages," Agnes said with pride.

"Basketball. Why isn't there a basketball court? It's the only modern sport my fellow sisters and I enjoy."

Agnes was caught off guard. "Um, I suppose we could add one, if we're willing to lose a few parking spaces over there. If the board and residents vote for it."

"Bah, you're too hobbled by your association's rules. I thought you were the nest mother."

"I am. But we live in condominiums. You must have rules."

"Vampires crave strong leadership," Mathilda said. "Whether it's a mother superior or a queen, their leader should be an authoritarian who rules with an iron claw and isn't afraid to mete out punishment. Vampires thrive when they have no say in how they're governed."

"Not these vampires." Agnes snorted with amusement. "You should see what it's like when you have to pass a special assessment. It's like World War Three."

"Because of lax leadership, the vampires here have become ungovernable. If I move here, we'll fix that."

Agnes tried to control her temper. "Mathilda, I've always treated you with the respect you deserve as an elder. I'll forever be grateful for the help you've given me over the centuries. But I'm my own vampire now. You must respect my world and its rules."

"Don't pout, dear. We'll find a way to work it out."

"Yeah, by you butting out," Agnes said under her breath.

Of course, with her preternatural hearing, Mathilda caught every word.

She hissed and bared her fangs, then turned it into a big fake smile.

"I was so hoping that you would welcome me here at your home. Just as I welcomed you into mine so many years ago."

"Of course you're welcome here," Agnes said with an equally strained smile. "I'd love to have you as a neighbor for eternity."

"We'll have so much fun!"

We'll see about that, I thought.

CHAPTER 13
LIKE A CLOWNFISH

Experts say people think of themselves as younger than their actual age. I guess that's the case for me, too. But every once in a while, I glimpse myself from afar with a big dose of critical judgment.

Like this morning, when I shuffled out of my house in my bathrobe and fuzzy slippers to pick up the daily newspaper that had been delivered to my driveway.

Yep, I felt like the middle-aged woman I really was.

Who still gets their news from a printed newspaper? I do. Who wears fuzzy yellow grandma slippers outside where neighbors can see you? I do.

But I'm not as old-fashioned as I seem. I know that everything nowadays needs to be encrypted and requires a password. Including my newspaper.

I once had a neighbor who occasionally swiped my paper from my driveway when his wasn't delivered. Not anymore.

You couldn't pry my paper from the concrete if you used a crowbar, let alone open and read it. Thanks to my magic.

This morning, I pulled my little, wrinkled password book from the pocket of my robe, found the one for my newspaper, and recited it aloud to unlock my magic and give me access to it.

See how current and techno-savvy I am?

When I returned inside, I opened *The Jellyfish Beach Journal* and took a sip of hot tea. The front page was dominated by a story about the downtown murders.

With Matt's byline, the story presented the facts as offered to him by the police. It didn't contain any of Matt's observations because he would never have shared them with the public. Instead, there was no mention of werewolves. The article made it sound as if Damian and Boris died as the result of a dispute of some sort with a third individual or individuals.

Though Matt and I knew what had really happened, our main theory was revenge killings by Dunott's brother. The only lead that seemed promising in Dunott's murder was the odd friendship Georgette described between her husband and restaurant owner Leticia Maldonado.

"I think it's time for your truth spell," Matt said.

I agreed. Like we had at Finnegans Wake Pub, we arrived in the late morning when El Pez Afortunado's employees were there, but it wasn't open yet for lunch.

We asked to speak with Leticia. We were not invited back to her office.

We stood beside the large aquarium that separated the bar area from the main dining room. I watched the Clownfish and

Damselfish swim listlessly among corals, hoping they didn't feel as frustrated as I did.

After ten minutes or so, Leticia came out of her office and greeted us graciously, though I could tell she wasn't pleased to see us. Her tall, slender frame, perfectly coiffed chestnut hair, and elegant pantsuit made me feel like a frumpy witch.

"How can I help you?" she asked. "I hope this isn't about the most recent murders. I know nothing about what happened or why. No one does. All of us on the boulevard are shocked and saddened."

It sounded like a well-rehearsed statement. Time to throw her off balance.

"Actually, we're here to ask you more about Pierre Dunott."

She frowned. "Okay. Please have a seat." We sat on stools around a high-top table next to the aquarium. "What do you want to know?"

"We spoke to his widow," Matt said. "She's quite fond of you and mentioned you comped their meals on a regular basis. She was quite oblivious to how abnormal that is."

"Yes, it was," Leticia said in a flat, angry voice. "It was part of her husband's shakedown of my business. I thought giving him envelopes of cash was sleazy, so he suggested free meals for perpetuity. And they sure took advantage of them. They came in a few times a week and ordered the best of everything. It was disgusting, all the food they wasted when the two pigs were too stuffed to eat."

The hatred radiated from her. The bitter tone with which she said "pigs" seemed like it had more behind it. I took an enormous risk.

"We've been told that Pierre was a philanderer," I said. "Did he think of himself as a real ladies' man?"

"Yes. When he came here without his wife, for lunch or late dinners after commission meetings, he would hit on the women at the bar."

Matt's eyes were wide and darted back and forth between Leticia and me.

"Did he, by any chance, hit on you?" I asked.

She seemed to withdraw, and her eyes became icy.

"He did. My recent divorce made him think I was fair game. I wasn't. His piggish ways were among the reasons I finally cut off their free meals. I couldn't bear to see him in here with his wife after he treated me so disgustingly."

Would the combination of the extortion and the sexual advances be enough to drive her to murder? Perhaps, especially if things had gone further than she was admitting.

"I would think whoever murdered him was the same person who killed Damian Connolly and Boris Jones," she said, trying to change the subject.

It was time to cast my truth spell.

"If that's true, it would make things a lot simpler," Matt said. "Besides, it's hard to imagine more than one murderer in our little town."

I hoped he continued to distract her while I enabled the spell and attempted to sprinkle the powder on her feet beneath the table. The small diameter of the high-top didn't help at all.

"Has there ever been more than one murder in a year here?" Leticia asked.

"Um, yes, unfortunately," Matt replied. It seemed like the murders increased when we started working together to solve them. "But this is a very safe place. The murders we've had weren't robberies or drug-related street crimes. They're more like crimes of passion. You know, the kinds of crimes that could happen anywhere."

I had sprinkled the powder while they were talking and whispered the incantation. The energy whooshed from me directly to Leticia.

I watched her carefully. She didn't yet have the animated look of those who were under the spell and had the sudden urge to unburden themselves.

"What was the tipping point between you and Dunott?" I asked. "Did he ever touch you?"

She looked at me with disgust that I had returned the questions to this unsavory topic.

"I'd rather not talk about it anymore."

This was not good. Was the spell working?

"I have to ask you again if there's anyone you suspect would have killed him."

"Like I told you before, Maddie Jong would be my choice."

The energy from my spell was drifting back to me, the way surf that crashes against a seawall flows back toward the sea.

"What about Fred Furman?"

"I don't know. I don't think so. He doesn't seem the type."

"What about you? Did you kill him?"

Her face turned dark, and she stood up abruptly.

"I've had enough of your rude behavior. I've told you all I know, and you guys are just a reporter and a botanica owner. Please leave now so I can prepare for the lunch service."

Even though she was angry, she remained poised.

"Thank you for your time," I said. "Sorry for being so rude. Have a nice day."

Before we left, I asked, "Can I still come in for a meal sometime?"

But she was already walking back to her office.

"Man, that sure was a bust," Matt said as we walked to his truck parked up the block on the boulevard. "Did the truth spell not work?"

"It didn't. I don't know why. It felt as if I had cast it correctly. Could she have resisted it somehow?"

"Did you sense magic in her?"

"No. As a werewolf, she's supernatural, but this spell works with werewolves. I didn't sense any other magical abilities in her."

"Well, what do you think? Did she do it?"

"Now that we know Maddie and Damian didn't do it, Leticia would be my best guess. She has a lot of anger in her. And I got the feeling she had her back up against the wall. Not just financially, but he was harassing her sexually."

"Yeah. But how do we know for sure she did it?"

"Did the police ever find a weapon, bullets, or spent casings?" I asked.

"I'm still waiting to hear. The fire made it almost impossible to get useful forensic evidence."

"Maybe magic can still help us. I'm going to talk to Angela and see if she has any thoughts on why my truth spell didn't work."

MATT DROPPED me off at the public library, a block away from the police station at the less-desirable end of the boulevard. I found Angela in her small office behind the check-out counter.

"How's the investigation going?" she asked me. "I heard there's a second loup-garou in town."

"Yes, and it's possible he's Dunott's twin brother, looking for revenge and following Matt and me around to kill our suspects."

"That sounds lazy. Can't he do his own investigation?"

"He must know how good Matt and I are."

She snorted derisively. How could such a sweet old lady be such a tiger at times?

"I need some magic advice," I said. "I used my truth spell on a suspect, and it had no effect at all."

"Remind me what truth spell you use."

I described it in great detail.

"Hmm, a bit primitive."

"It's always worked for me."

"I have a better one I can teach you. No powder-sprinkling required."

"I'd appreciate that. Unfortunately, our prime suspect will not give me another opportunity to speak with her."

"You might be surprised."

"It really bothers me that my spell didn't work. Do you have any ideas why? The suspect is a werewolf but has no magical abilities that I can sense. And I know my spell works on werewolves."

"She might not have magical abilities, but she might have had magic. A charm or amulet, perhaps."

"Wouldn't I have sensed it?"

"Not necessarily. If she held the charm in her hand, and all the magic flowed directly into her with none escaping, you probably wouldn't have sensed it."

"I don't know," I said. "I'm pretty sensitive with magic."

"With black magic, too?"

"Of course."

"Black-magic charms and amulets work the way I just described. If you're not specifically looking to detect the magic, and none escapes into the air, you won't sense it."

"Wow. Are you telling me my mother is involved with Leticia Maldonado?"

"Your mother is the only game in town when it comes to black magic. Perhaps Leticia sought your mother to give her extra power so she could kill Dunott."

I needed a moment to let that thought seep in.

"It doesn't mean your mother has anything to do with the murders," Angela added. "Only that Leticia sought magical help from her."

Believe me, I'm usually fast to draw the worst conclusions about my birth mother, but we hadn't seen any evidence of her involvement. Still, Angela's hypothesis meant I had to look into it further.

Which meant dealing with my mother, who has been insisting I join her coven, or cult, under the threat of death.

"What if Leticia had a white-magic charm, and I simply didn't detect it?" I asked.

"Who did she get it from? There aren't many white-magic

witches around here anymore. They've all been forced to join the coven. Did you give her the charm? I know I didn't."

"Good point."

"Sorry, I couldn't hear you."

A group of elementary-school kids had been dropped off at the library before I arrived. Screams and laughter were filling the building.

Angela closed her eyes and motioned with her hands. A blast of magic flew out the office door.

Suddenly, the cacophony was silenced.

"See?" She smiled. "Librarians don't need to use fear to maintain quiet."

When I left the library, the kids were all seated at tables studiously reading. They even seemed to be enjoying it.

CHAPTER 14
WORKED LIKE A CHARM

"Who cares if she got a charm from your mother?" Matt asked when I called him. "You need to stay away from that woman."

"We need to find out what kind of charm, amulet, or other item Leticia used to foil my spell. She doesn't know I'm a witch, or that I was casting a spell upon her. She must have gotten it for general protection from Dunott, which allowed her to murder him."

"What if it was simply to protect herself from a guy who was harassing her?"

"That's the point. We need to know why she got it and what she used it for."

"It seems like you're going off on a tangent."

"It could give us the evidence we need to confirm if Leticia is the murderer," I said, trying to hide my anger.

"You sound awfully adamant."

"I am. And I have an additional agenda. I haven't heard

anything from my mother or her cult for weeks, while the magical progress bar on my invitation to join shows that time is running out. I want to test the waters."

"What if she's forgotten about you? You'll be saying, 'Hey, Ruth. Remember your death threat to me?' And who says she would tell you the truth about helping Leticia? It's not as if you can use your truth spell on her."

"Low blow. Look, I have a gut feeling that I need to talk to her. And I think it will surprise her enough that she'll say more than she ought to."

"You're not going to see her in person, are you?"

"Of course not. Evil sorceresses are people you only want to text with. Especially if they've been threatening to kill you."

After we ended our call, I stared at my phone, trying to compose a text message. Deciding how to address her had always been awkward. I refused to call her "Mom." That title belonged to my adoptive mother who had raised me. "Mother" was technically correct, but still seemed too intimate. Her real name was Ophelia Lawthorne, but after years of committing evil deeds, she went by the alias of Ruth Bent.

"Dear Ruth," I said aloud as I typed.

I deleted "dear."

"Did you, by any chance, give a charm or amulet to a woman named Leticia Maldonado?"

I left out the fact that Leticia was a werewolf just in case Ruth hadn't known. After sending the text, I stared at the screen, waiting for a reply, as if my mother were a teenager with a hand always on her phone.

Meows in stereo came from Brenda and Bubba, staring at me from their feeding area in the kitchen. I got the message.

After I fed them, I fed myself some old leftovers. The cats got the better end of the deal.

When I stepped out of the kitchen, I got a rude surprise.

"You didn't answer my text," I said to my mother, who was seated on the living room couch.

"I'm answering it now."

"How did you get into my house?"

"I defeated the security wards in your yard and used an unlocking spell on your door. Your wards were pathetically weak."

"Apparently."

"You could use some magic lessons," she said in a patronizing tone. "I've heard you're being taught by a mage, but I can teach you more in one lesson than she could in a lifetime."

"I see your narcissism is stronger than ever."

"So is my magic. If you don't believe me, I can show you."

"That's not necessary. I was only wondering if you gave any magic to Leticia."

"Let me guess. You tried to enchant her, and it didn't work?"

I nodded.

"Your pathetically weak magic was no match for my simple charm."

"Thank you for finally answering my question. Why did you give her the charm?"

"Because she asked for one. And paid me handsomely."

"I thought you gave up your fee-for-service model and were living off the dues from your brainwashed followers."

"I never turn down easy cash."

"But why did she want the charm?"

"It's none of your business. My clients deserve their privacy."

"Your power as a sorceress has made you famous," I said, feigning sincerity. "Don't you want the word to spread even more?"

"She came to me to protect herself from a werewolf. She didn't realize that I knew she was a werewolf herself. The other werewolf must be quite a powerful one."

"I guess your charm worked, because she was able to kill the other werewolf, most likely when they were both in human form."

Ruth smiled. "Good. And it defeated your magic, too. What spell did you use on her?"

"My truth-telling spell. I wanted her to admit she was the murderer."

"My charm worked like a charm," Ruth said, cackling.

"What kind of spell did you put in the charm?"

"Oh, you're curious about my magic now? Like I've always told you, black magic is the way to go."

"I simply want to make adjustments to improve my spell."

"To answer your question, my spell for the charm used nothingness."

"What do you mean, you used nothing?" I asked, frustrated.

"I said nothing-*ness*. It's a foundation of black magic."

"What does it mean?"

"Nothingness is the opposite of reality, cancelling out existence. It's the void past the edges of the universe. It causes death, decay, disintegration. Your spell's magic was sucked away by the nothingness. Any supernatural creature that attacked the holder of the charm would lose their magic or superpowers."

It made sense in the abstract, but I couldn't imagine how such a force would be practical and how to get it into a spell.

"Doesn't it have an effect on whoever holds the charm?" I asked. "Because she's a werewolf, after all."

"Yes. I put some shielding magic in it to protect the user, but eventually the user would be weakened and sickened."

"That's an awfully big negative."

She snorted derisively. "All power comes with a cost. But the charm worked, didn't it? It defeated your spell. And it sounds like it enabled Letty, or whatever her name is, to kill that werewolf."

"Yes, that's what it sounds like."

"Interested in learning the spell I used?"

"No, thank you. I appreciate your telling me about it, though."

I stood to signal it was time for her to leave. She didn't take the hint.

"You're living on borrowed time, dearie." She picked up the invitation to join her coven, which I'd left lying on the side table. "See, your deadline is fast approaching."

The "deadline" was a thick line printed on the card with magic ink. The line grew in length from left to right, like a progress bar on a computer. It was getting awfully close to the right edge of the card. I didn't know if I would automatically die when the line reached its end, or if someone would kill me. I assumed it would be the latter.

But the threat was clear: I must join mother's coven or die.

"Are you skeptical of my threat?" she asked. "You saw

how much power I put into a tiny charm. I've grown much more dangerous since the last time I tried to kill you."

I'll say one thing about this woman: she can be completely honest when she wants to be.

"I don't want to join your coven," I said in a voice meeker than I had intended. "I wouldn't make a good black-magic witch."

"It doesn't really matter, as long as you pay your monthly dues. If you pay for the year in advance, you'll get a big discount."

"How about if I don't join but pay your dues, anyway? Like protection money."

Just like the business owners of downtown had been paying. How ironic.

"It's not all about money," she replied. "I also enjoy having total dominance over my witches."

I shrugged. "I was offering you easy money."

"You're full of nonsense. You have no intention of paying me. I'm not stupid."

She was angry. Note to self: do not anger an evil psychopath.

I caught a whiff of sulfur and brimstone. It probably wasn't her cologne; it was probably black magic brewing.

"Please don't hurt me," I said, instantly regretting showing weakness. The problem was, she knew some really painful spells.

I quickly worked on a protection spell.

"I don't want to intimidate you into joining my coven like I did with the others. I want you to join willingly."

There was no way I would join willingly, but I kept my mouth shut as her gathering magic made my scalp tingle.

"You need to learn about the liberating power of black magic," she continued. "Notice how easily my spell cuts through your silly little protection bubble."

My vision clouded, and my head spun.

"Like butter." Her words sounded far away.

I braced for pain, but instead I went into a waking dream.

My living room had disappeared, and I was now in the intensive care unit of the regional hospital. It was where I had worked years ago until burnout forced me out of my job and into home-health nursing.

I walked down the hall, past the nurses' station, and stopped at the nearest patient room. The hiss of a ventilator and the myriad beeps and clicks of the various patient-monitoring machines faded.

Suddenly, the patients in the two beds gained consciousness and got out of bed, smiling at me. They removed their IV leads, and each hugged me, a man, and a woman, whispering their gratitude into my ears. Then they strolled out of the room like they'd never been sick at all.

"Hold the backs of your gowns closed," I called after them. "Your butts are showing."

I went from room to room, and the moment I entered each one, the patients were miraculously cured. How was this happening? All I did was get near them, and they leaped out of bed in perfect health.

After I visited every room in the unit, I found myself in the hospital's cancer institute. I visited every patient, and each one left their beds cancer-free, hugging me in gratitude. Even the patients recovering from surgery were completely healed in an instant.

The realization struck me that magic was responsible. *My* magic. And it went far beyond anything I dreamed was possible with magic.

Just like when you have a dream and a part of your mind knows it's only a dream, I knew what I was experiencing wasn't real. This was being orchestrated by my mother to make a point.

That her kind of magic could do profound good despite my preconceptions of black magic only being used for harm.

This demonstration was all a lie, I told myself. She's trying to fool me. Yet my denials were unable to snap me out of this hallucination.

And every patient I encountered seemed so real.

"God bless you, dear," said the elderly African American woman who was hugging me. "I'll always be grateful for your healing touch."

I'd had countless patients thank me during my career, but none as fervently as these. Because these had been healed through the miracle of magic.

I went through the entire hospital healing every patient. It must have taken hours, but it felt like mere minutes had passed. Throughout it all, I never saw a doctor, nurse, or any other worker.

Until I reached the lobby. It was filled with the entire staff of the hospital, all applauding and cheering as if I were the world's greatest hero. I recognized the members of my former team, as well as doctors and administrators.

They gushed with their appreciation for me, way more than

they ever had when I worked here. It was the kind of gratitude everybody craves but rarely receives.

I wished this wasn't a dream and could go on forever.

"Then you should learn black magic," said my mother, her voice still sounding far away.

"You're trying to trick me," I said.

Now I was outside, standing in the ambulance bay. An ambulance backed in, and as the paramedics lowered the gurney to the ground, the patient jumped up and walked away.

"This is lovely wish fulfillment," I said, "but I'm not naïve."

"Being skeptical makes you feel wise, but you're being stupid," my mother said from somewhere unseen. "You'd be perfectly capable of achieving results like this with black magic if you had the skill and the desire. You see, this magic is called black by its detractors, none of who know how to use it."

"Black magic comes from evil," I said.

"Who cares where it comes from if it achieves good?"

"I've never heard of it doing good."

"Because when it does good, they call it something else. And, yes, many black-magic makers love using it to give their enemies embarrassing rashes, and stuff like that. But you can use it as you wish."

"I'm still skeptical," I said, suddenly back in my living room, standing where I'd been when I tried to give Ruth the hint to leave.

"I know you don't trust or believe me but think about it. Quickly." She pointed at the progress bar on the invitation. "You're running out of time. It's your choice: get all the power you secretly crave or die. It's very simple."

Finally, she stood up and walked to the front door.

"You're welcome for me not smoking in your house."

"Right. Thanks for breaking in and hijacking my brain while not smoking."

"Any time, dearie. Until your deadline, that is."

She went out the door, and no trace of her magic was left behind.

I was angry now that the euphoria of my dream was gone. I felt manipulated and violated. She had taken advantage of my instinct to help others that had led me into nursing and the desire for acknowledgment that medical professionals rarely receive. She amplified them beyond believability into ridiculousness. Did she really think I was that gullible?

Still, I couldn't erase the memory of the joy I'd felt healing those patients.

The invitation card levitated from the end table and hovered in front of me. The "deadline" had inched further to the right.

CHAPTER 15
ACKNEY TREATMENT

Transitioning from working nights caring for vampires to working normal daytime hours had been difficult for me. I still saw some vampire patients, like my visit to Mrs. Sneiderman last night, so I didn't get to bed until 1:30 a.m.

I was sound asleep when Matt's call awakened me at 6:30 a.m. When I saw it was his number, I silenced the phone and went back to sleep. I knew he'd forgive me.

The phone buzzed from a text message. I tossed it onto a chair on the other side of the room. Where it buzzed again ten minutes later.

By now, both cats realized their human's sleeping time was over. Bubba sat on the nightstand, staring at me and meowing. Brenda lay on my chest and occasionally batted my chin.

"Okay, okay," I mumbled as I resigned myself to another day of feeling sleep deprived.

After feeding the cats, I found my phone and read Matt's

texts. Apparently, he'd finally located Dunott's personal assistant and had convinced him to meet us for coffee.

In forty-five minutes from now.

I texted Matt that I would be there, a little late, and jumped in the shower, rushing to get ready. There's nothing like a little panic to help you wake up.

The coffee shop was a block south of Jellyfish Beach Boulevard, in what used to be a home built in the 1890s. Matt and our interviewee were already at a table, sipping coffee from tall mugs.

They stood when I approached, and Matt introduced me to Greg Ackney, a hulking giant with a shaved head. He looked more like a bodyguard than an assistant. He wore a black blazer over a black T-shirt that strained to cover his massive pecs.

"Mr. Ackney was Mr. Dunott's aide in his legal work, as well as in his duties on the commission," Matt explained.

I hadn't realized the part-time commissioners needed aides. In any event, I was eager to hear if Ackney had any valuable information.

"This place is where Mr. Dunott and I spent our days," Ackney said in a deep Southern accent. "It was like our office."

"There you are, Greg!" A woman in her forties, who had come from the kitchen area, gave Ackney a hug and a kiss on the cheek. "I haven't seen you since the tragedy. How are you holding up, love?"

"I'm okay, Judy. Thanks for asking. How are *you* holding up? You and Mr. Dunott went back quite a ways."

"I'm missing him hard," she said, wiping a tear from her eye. "I hope you will keep coming here every day. Sorry for interrupting," she said to Matt and me before squeezing Ackney's shoulder and returning to the kitchen.

"Judy's the owner. She was a big supporter and great friend of Mr. Dunott's," Ackney said to us.

Matt gave me a knowing look, meaning the owner wasn't a victim of the shakedowns.

"Mr. Dunott didn't have an actual office?" I asked.

Ackney shook his head. "When he wasn't here, he worked out of his home."

"Did he meet with people at his home, as well as here?"

"Yeah, but only people he knew well."

"Like Fred Furman? Or Leticia Maldonado?"

"Not Furman. He's a jerk. Leticia came by his home office occasionally. They were friends."

Leticia hadn't talked about Dunott as if they were friends.

"Were they, perhaps, more than friends?" I asked.

Greg smiled. "Mr. Dunott behaved like a consummate professional."

"Did any other local business owners visit his home office?" Matt asked.

"Not really. I think Stuart McDougall might have gone there a couple of times."

"His political opponent?"

"Yeah. It was about some legal stuff. They're both attorneys, you know."

"Yeah. Now, the police must have asked you this, but do you know of anyone making threats against Mr. Dunott?"

Ackney laughed. "All the time."

"Serious, actionable threats?"

"The Asian chick who owns the biker bar threatened to kill

him. The other people just promised to sue him or get him kicked off the commission. I would still want to work for Mr. Dunott, even if he wasn't a commissioner. But now that he's dead, I'm out of a job, with no prospects."

"We've looked into Maddie Jong," Matt said. "She had bad intentions, but it doesn't look like she killed Mr. Dunott. If you had to pick someone else most likely to be the murderer, who would it be?"

Ackney clasped his hands, deep in thought.

"Leticia Maldonado," he replied. "I got the vibe that things really went south between them."

"Any specifics you can provide?" I asked.

"The day before he died, he got a call from her. He was shouting, and I could hear her shouting on the other end. Mr. Dunott said he was going to shut her down if she didn't do what he wanted. That's all I remember."

"Thank you," I said.

Matt thanked him, too, and wished him luck before we said our goodbyes.

As soon as we left the coffee shop, Matt and I locked eyes.

"Leticia," I said.

"Yeah. I want to speak with her again."

"Not now. She's still mad at me. Maybe we have enough information now to share it with Shortle and put this case behind us. If only the second loup-garou wasn't out there."

"You know, something in the coffee shop bothered me," Matt said. "That whole scene between the owner, Judy, and Ackney seemed unnatural. Like they were putting on a performance for our benefit."

"I think you're paranoid."

"I covered Dunott's funeral service for the newspaper the other day. I saw the two of them consoling each other. Just now, they acted like they hadn't seen each other since before the murder."

"Some people express their emotions flamboyantly," I said. "The fact we were watching might have amplified their performance."

"Yeah. I guess. In the meantime, I want to talk to McDougall again. I'm curious about why he visited Dunott's home office."

Matt called McDougall's firm and asked for him.

"He won't take your call," I said.

Matt just smiled and continued to wait on hold.

"Okay, I'll try tomorrow then. Thank you." He hung up. "The receptionist said he's in court today. That's good. It will be easier to ambush him in a public setting. Let's head for the courthouse."

The main Crab County Courthouse was in Mullet City, about an hour away. But there was also the smaller East County Courthouse here in Jellyfish Beach, which mostly handled civil cases. That's where McDougall would be.

There was only one hearing in session today, so Matt and I waited patiently outside the courtroom until people filed out.

"There he is," Matt whispered as he jumped to his feet and stepped into McDougall's path.

"Oh, no," McDougall said. "Not you again."

"Sir, can you tell me why you visited Pierre Dunott's home office recently?"

The attorney stopped with genuine confusion on his face.

"His home office," Matt repeated. "You two were opponents in the last election, which makes it odd."

"Ahh, now I remember. Dunott did some consulting work for my firm regarding a real-estate rezoning request before the city. I must have been dropping off paperwork for him."

"Why not have an assistant do that?"

"Because I used to live on the next street over from him. I stopped on my way home."

"Okay. Was there any rancor between you two after the election?"

"Not at all. Pierre took the election much more seriously than I did. And spent more money on campaigning. I'll admit that he wanted the job more than I did, and I wasn't that upset when I lost."

I watched his face carefully. He seemed to be telling the truth. And no, I wasn't going to cast the truth-telling spell on him here in the courthouse hallway.

"Did he harass your law firm after his reelection?"

McDougall smiled wryly. "No, he left us alone, unlike those other businesses. He should have been sued for that."

"Someone solved the problem extrajudicially," Matt said. "Who do you suspect that might be?"

"Oh, I don't know. There are a few rough characters who own businesses in our town. Now, do you mind getting out of my way? I need to get back to my office."

Matt thanked him and stepped aside, away from the stream of people leaving the courtroom. His phone rang. It was too noisy with all the voices and footfalls on the marble floors beneath the high ceiling, so I couldn't hear his side of the conversation.

Finally, he put his phone away and came over to me. He was frowning.

"That was my contact at the local FBI office. The police did find shell casings and bullets in Dunott's bedroom. The FBI performed the ballistics work for them. My contact said the casings came from a nine-millimeter pistol, most likely a Glock."

"So?"

"The police will have to find the gun to match them. But the weird finding is about the bullets. Normally, in a fire like that, the lead bullets would have melted. In this case, they only melted slightly, because they weren't made of lead. They were silver."

"Silver bullets? Just like you joked about with Shortle," I said.

"Yep. Like the hitmen had in case Dunott shifted."

"Do you realize what this means? The shooter couldn't have been a werewolf. Even if a human loaded the gun with bullets, a werewolf would have had physical issues holding the gun and firing it."

"If you're certain Leticia is a werewolf, then she couldn't be the murderer. None of these people we've suspected could be, nor could his wife, who you said was a shifter. Unless they had a human do it. Like another hitman."

"Wait a minute. Leticia had a black-magic charm she got from my mother, which was supposed to protect her from a loup-garou. It prevented my truth spell from working on her. Maybe, just maybe, it could protect her from silver?"

"I don't know," Matt said. "Haven't you told me that were-wolves' aversion to silver is fundamental?"

"There's only one way to find out for sure. You wanted to speak with her again. Bring some silver with you."

"You've got to be kidding. What kind of interview would that be? It'd be like trying to interview a vampire while you're holding a crucifix."

"All we need to know is if she has an aversion to silver."

"Okay, okay."

OF COURSE, Leticia wouldn't agree to meet with Matt, even though it was I who had been rude to her. So, we did the McDougall strategy and ambushed her. We arrived early in the morning and waited outside the restaurant until she pulled up in her BMW.

"Morning, Ms. Maldonado," Matt said, rushing up to her car as she was getting out. "I just had a quick question for you."

"I told you I don't want to talk to you."

"You're talking to me now. Is it really that bad?"

"Get out of my way, or I'm calling the police."

"I wanted to ask you why you went to Dunott's house if he was harassing you."

"I went there for a meeting at his request *before* he began harassing me."

"Multiple times?"

"Get out of my way."

"Can you explain this photo of you?" Matt asked as he thrust a manilla envelope at her.

It contained a thin cardboard sheet that would make you

believe an 8x10-inch photo print was in the envelope. A sterling-silver chain necklace of mine was also inside.

She moved her arm as if she intended to knock his hand out of the way. But something made her hesitate.

"Of course, we would never publish this photo," Matt said.

She grabbed the envelope.

Then yanked her hand away, her body doubling over. She gasped with pain.

Yep, she had an aversion to silver.

"Go away!" she shrieked. "I'm calling the police."

This werewolf couldn't have handled or fired the gun that was loaded with silver bullets.

Did that mean she was innocent? Or had she hired someone to kill Dunott?

Unfortunately, that was a question I didn't believe we could answer. It would be up to the police to search her phone and other electronic records to see if she'd been in contact with known bad guys.

I explained my reasoning to Matt when we got in his truck.

"Yeah, I think you're right," he said.

"Except there's something else I'm wondering about."

"There's always something else."

"Seriously. The hitmen Maddie and her group hired had a gun loaded with silver bullets. How common are silver bullets?"

"I'm willing to bet you won't find them in the firearms counter at Mega-Mart."

"Exactly. So, it's not a great stretch to postulate that the person who cast the silver bullets for the hitmen might have also supplied them to whoever killed Dunott."

"You're right!" Matt exclaimed, slapping his thigh. "We need to talk to Maddie. I don't care how much she denies hiring the hitmen, we've got to get her to tell us who made the silver bullets."

"I'm sure she didn't give them to the hitmen herself."

"Of course not. But she must know where the bullets came from."

It seemed so simple.

Little did we know that Matt's police scanner would crackle to life after midnight with radio chatter about a violent murder at a restaurant on Jellyfish Beach Boulevard.

A restaurant named El Pez Afortunado.

CHAPTER 16
SILVER BULLETS

Detective Shortle was unusually communicative when Matt and I arrived at the crime scene. I got the feeling that she was at her wit's end with this investigation and no longer saw us as interfering, because she could use all the help she could get.

Leticia's BMW was in the same spot she had parked it in behind her restaurant when we ambushed her yesterday. But it looked like a peanut shell that had been cracked open. The driver's door had been torn from the frame and tossed several feet away.

The body lay on the asphalt near the car, covered with a tarp.

"The manager said Ms. Maldonado was the last to leave after closing the restaurant," Shortle told us.

"How did you find the manager?" Matt asked.

"He called us. The victim hit the panic button on her key

fob, and it's connected to the restaurant's security system. The company called the manager."

My heart sank as I imagined how terrifying Leticia's final moments must have been. Did her charm fail to protect her, or did she not have it with her?

"The murderer chased her to her car?" I asked.

"That's highly likely," Shortle replied.

"Was she shot, or . . . something else?"

"Like the last two killings. Blunt-force trauma and slashing wounds."

A sleepy-faced young man in shorts and a T-shirt exited the building.

"Um, ma'am, I cued up the video footage," he said to Shortle.

She turned and followed him inside. Matt and I scurried after them, though I knew we'd be ordered to stay out. We weren't.

In an office connected to the kitchen, the manager sat at a computer. The screen was filled with a shot of the parking lot behind the restaurant.

"This camera had the best angle," he explained.

Shortle stood behind him and watched as the video showed Leticia walking from the building toward her car. She got in and closed the door.

Then, the door popped open at an odd angle and detached from the car, flying a few yards away. Leticia exited the car as if she had been violently yanked, but a dark shadow obscured her, blocking the camera's view of what was happening.

The shadow moved away, revealing her body on the ground.

The camera had captured the entire attack, but it didn't show the assailant, which, I assumed, had been the loup-garou. Did that mean supernatural creatures couldn't be recorded by video?

"Why don't we see the attacker?" I asked, curious about how Shortle would rationalize it.

She gave me a penetrating look. "I thought you could tell me. When weird stuff happens, you always seem to know about it."

"We're only here because Matt heard the call on his police scanner."

"At the last murder scene, there was no security camera at all," she said. "Regarding the incident before that, at Finnegans Wake Pub, there was only low-quality footage. But just like this, it didn't show the assailant. Does this have anything to do with that black magic you're always talking about?"

"I don't think these murders had anything to do with black magic."

"Look," the manager said. "Someone else is leaving the building."

"Rewind it," Shortle said.

When the video replayed, at a slower speed, it showed a large, long-haired man walking briskly from the building. His head was turned away from the camera, as if he knew it might be there.

The figure looked a lot like the man I saw leaving The Ripped Tide after Boris was killed.

Though I couldn't see his face, something about the man's size and long hair reminded me of Pierre Dunott.

In other words, this could very well be his twin, here to

exact revenge for his brother's murder. That we might have led him to Leticia—a possibility I had been trying not to think about—washed over me.

"Have you been investigating Leticia Maldonado for Pierre Dunott's murder?" I asked Shortle.

"You know I can't comment on that."

"I'm asking because the people killed since his murder were among those Matt and I suspected. Except for Boris Jones, who died while the killer was trying to get to Maddie Jong."

Shortle looked at me strangely. I guessed it was because she had suspected the same people.

"We spoke to Dunott's widow, and she mentioned Dunott had a brother, a twin brother. I think he might have come to town to get revenge for Dunott's murder."

"How would he know who the suspects are?" Shortle asked defensively. "Is he yet another amateur Sherlock Holmes like you guys?"

"Maybe."

"Hey, I'm a professional journalist," Matt said.

"Someone at the police department could have leaked information," I said.

"Or someone you know told him," Shortle retorted.

I believed now more than ever, but couldn't mention to Shortle, that the loup-garou had learned about the suspects by reading our minds. The timing of the murders coincided too perfectly with whenever Matt and I grew more certain about a particular suspect.

Still, the twin brother should have figured out by now that following our hunches was not an effective way to punish the real murderer. Our hunches had been wrong.

And innocent people died as a result.

Matt pulled me aside and said, "It's not our fault that Leticia died."

"Were you reading my mind?"

"No. I was just going through a guilt trip."

"It makes me want to find the actual murderer even more, even if it's just to stop these innocent people from being killed."

"The investigative process is all about eliminating suspects. It's not our fault if someone else literally eliminates them."

"That someone is a loup-garou who needs to be stopped. The only way to do it is with a silver bullet. We know one hitman had some. He's dead now and we'll never be able to find his partner again. We know that Dunott's murderer used them. We need to find out where you can buy silver bullets around here and maybe the seller can tell us who the buyers were."

"I called Maddie last night and asked her if she knew where to buy silver bullets," Matt said. "She played dumb. So I said I heard that a recently deceased hitman had some. She swore at me and hung up. I don't think I'm welcome at The Ripped Tide anymore."

"What a shame," I said with maximum sarcasm.

"Then I searched the internet for silver bullets."

"You did? I should have thought to do that."

"Yeah. And I found a bunch of them. They're mostly sold as collectibles. I even found a few places that sold real silver bullets you can shoot. But they're really expensive, as you can imagine. Some gun hobbyists cast their own bullets, so there could be someone local who made them in his garage."

"How do we find this person?"

"I don't know. I guess we should start by asking at a gun shop."

We each went home to catch a couple of hours of sleep before we had to go to work. Matt agreed to pick me up when I took my lunch break at the botanica.

Jellyfish Beach wasn't too small to have its own gun shop. It was located several blocks from downtown, so we could be reasonably certain the owner wasn't a werewolf.

"Yeah, I know several people who cast their own bullets. I do, too, on occasion," said the elderly owner whose thick eyeglass lenses indicated he might not be the best marksman anymore.

"Do you know anyone who makes silver bullets?" Matt asked. "Real bullets for shooting, not for displaying on a shelf."

"You mean for killing werewolves?" He laughed.

"Yes," Matt said, without a trace of a smile.

"Brian Bartman does. I don't know if he sells them, though. I'll give you his phone number."

It took several tries to get through to Bartman, but Matt arranged a meeting for the early evening. Business was slow that afternoon at the botanica, so I wound up the ancient grandfather clock and closed the shop early, putting extra power into the security wards, just in case my mother had mischief up her sleeves.

The moment I got home, I was set upon by my hungry housemates, who acted like they were starving even though I had returned an hour early.

"Why do you always feed the cats before me?" Tony asked. "I'm your witch's familiar."

"Because they've been with me longer than you have," I

said as I set out two plates with cat food. "They're my babies. You're my associate."

"Sounds kinda cold if you ask me. 'Associate.' It's like I'm a sales associate at Mega-Mart. I help you develop spells. I connect with you telepathically."

"You're a cold-blooded lizard. I can't bring myself to call you my baby."

"I was thinking more like your partner."

I looked at the four-foot-long green iguana. He had a sad expression, which I hadn't thought lizard faces were capable of.

"Okay. You're my partner. Now, let's go to the garage, and I'll feed you your iguana chow."

"Your partner's got to eat in the garage?"

"Those are the rules, partner."

When I returned from the garage, the doorbell rang. I knew instantly it had to be my handlers from the Friends of Cryptids Society.

"We've come to speak with you about silver bullets," Mrs. Lupis said.

"How did you know about our appointment tonight?"

"We know the original murder victim was killed by silver bullets," Mr. Lopez said. "Therefore, it stands to reason that you would investigate where they came from."

"We anticipate you'll consider buying some for self-protection," said Mrs. Lupis. "We don't think that's a good idea."

"I hadn't thought about it just yet because I don't have a gun. But now that you mention it, I think it *is* a good idea. Matt has a gun."

"We don't want you to kill the loup-garou."

"It's better than getting killed ourselves."

"We want you to capture him," Mr. Lopez said.

"You've got to be kidding. It's one of the most dangerous monsters there is. It's not like catching a munuane or a harmless chimera."

"We've never had the opportunity to examine a loup-garou in a laboratory. You only need to disable him using your immobility or sleep spells."

"You sound certain those spells will work. What if they don't? I'll be torn to pieces."

"Then we resort to Plan B," said Mrs. Lupis.

"Shoot it with a silver bullet?"

"No. That would be Plan C, the last resort. We haven't devised a Plan B yet."

"Wonderful."

"If you come into contact with the loup-garou, please let us know immediately," Mr. Lopez said. "We'll have your back."

"With what?"

"Plan B. As soon as we have one. But try to immobilize the creature with your magic first."

They nodded curtly and walked from my porch to the street, where no car was waiting. I watched them walk down the street until they turned the corner and disappeared from view.

I wondered where they went each time after visiting me. To an office? To their respective homes or a home they shared? Into a burrow in the ground? I didn't even know what species they were, now that they had admitted they were cryptids themselves.

Perhaps it was better if I didn't know.

BRIAN BARTMAN's garage was part metalworking shop and part foundry. Metal signs with strange arcane symbols hung on the walls. I knew it wouldn't be wise to ask him what they meant.

The man was in his fifties, short with massive upper-body strength, skinny legs, and knobby knees beneath his shorts. He squinted at us while we introduced ourselves.

"You say you want silver bullets?" he asked.

"Yes." Matt gave a forced laugh. "For a friend of mine who's a collector."

"But you want actual bullets in cartridges with primers. Bullets that you can shoot."

"Yes."

"For killing werewolves?"

"Ha, no."

"Yes, you do. That's why I make 'em. I have hundreds of rounds in case werewolves become a problem around here. I'd make even more, but silver is expensive. It's got to be ninety-nine percent pure if you want to guarantee kill shots."

Little did he know werewolves *were already* a problem around here. Or maybe he did. I hoped he was just a fantasist and not aware of our supernatural population.

"I also make explosive rounds for zombies, because you never know when there might be an outbreak."

"What are these?" Matt asked, examining a pile of extra-large cartridges.

"Fifty-caliber, armor-piercing rounds for kraken. Living on the ocean like we do, you got to be prepared for marauding kraken attacking boats."

"That, you do," Matt replied. "What about vampires? Are you prepared for them?"

"Sure am. People think you got to kill 'em with wooden stakes. Nope, metal will work, too." He pointed to a bundle of sharpened metal rods in the corner. "The key is to keep the stake or rod lodged in the vampire's heart until the shriveled organ disintegrates. I'm trying to develop a bullet that would do the same thing."

"Sounds promising."

"Yeah. I think of myself as an innovator."

"Do you sell a lot of your creations?" I asked.

"No," he said, chagrined. "People laugh at me. But when we have a monster apocalypse, they'll come running to me. You can bet on it. That's why I stay well-stocked. What caliber silver bullets do you need?"

Matt struggled to remember. "For a .38."

"I got plenty of those. One hundred bucks each."

Matt gulped. "I'll take just three. I'm a good shot."

I handed Matt a hundred bucks. "Make it four, just in case."

Brian shook his head like we were foolish and gave Matt a small box after he paid him.

"Have you sold any other silver bullets lately?" I asked.

"Funny you ask. I had two customers recently after almost a year of none at all."

"Can you tell me who the customers were?"

"Nope. Sorry. My customers deserve their privacy. Besides, I don't even ask their names if they don't volunteer them, and I only take payment in cash."

"Can you tell me *anything* about them?"

"One was a man who looked a little shady, to be honest. The other was a woman. A pretty one."

"Can you describe the woman?"

"I'd rather not, except I'll say she was around your age. And she didn't know jack about firearms!" He chuckled at that.

We thanked him, and on the ride home, Matt said he should have bought more silver bullets.

"I'm not really a good shot. But they're so expensive!"

"Mr. Lopez and Mrs. Lupis want me to capture the loup-garou if my magic is strong enough. But we might need the bullets if it isn't."

"I guess the male customer was the hitman who died."

"Yes," I said. "I wonder who the woman was."

"Brian said she was forty-something and pretty. Like you."

"You know it wasn't me."

"That also describes Judy."

"Who?"

"The owner of the coffeeshop where Ackney and Dunott spent so much time."

"There are many forty-something women in Jellyfish Beach. The one thing we know is that she wasn't a werewolf or loup-garou, which, I guess, rules out half the town."

"Then who was it? She could be Dunott's murderer."

"Or she gave the bullets to the murderer."

I sighed. "We're stuck in a dead end. We know nothing, except that we were wrong about our previous suspects. Maddie didn't do it, though she's guilty of conspiracy to commit murder."

"And it's not our responsibility to prove that," Matt said. "We only need to find the actual murderer."

"Must you always protect Maddie?"

"I'm protecting my favorite watering hole."

"It wasn't Furman, Damian, or Leticia, either. All we know now is that the shooter wasn't a werewolf. Still, one or more werewolves could have been involved in the plot."

"I wonder why Furman wasn't killed by Dunott's brother. We suspected Furman for a little while."

"We did, but the brother probably hadn't arrived in town yet. But that gives me an idea. Now that we're supposed to capture the loup-garou—"

"Not we," Matt said. "*You.* Your bosses gave you the assignment."

"I thought we were in this together. I thought you cared about me."

"Don't manipulate me."

"You're more scared of an overgrown werewolf than in love with me. But anyway, Dunott's brother doesn't know about the silver bullets. So, if we pretend that we suspect Furman, the brother will go after him like he did with our other suspects. We could set a trap."

"Leaving poor Furman as bait?"

"It sounds heartless when you put it that way," I replied. "But, yes."

"And how do we find the murderer?"

"Since the individuals who wanted Dunott dead are werewolves, we have two possibilities. One, they hired another hitman or hitmen. I wouldn't know where to start to find them. Since Furman is the head of the merchant association, he might know. The other possibility is that Dunott was murdered for a completely different reason than what we've assumed."

"Ah. That would make sense."

"The problem is, how do we find out what that motive might have been?"

"Remember," Matt said, "all we can do is look for suspects. And then eliminate them."

"Before the loup-garou eliminates them."

We brooded in silence.

CHAPTER 17

WOULDN'T BE CAUGHT UNDEAD HERE

I was walking through the Squid Tower lobby on my way to the weekly creative-writing workshop, when Agnes ran from the elevator to intercept me, desperate to talk.

"Missy," she said, "I feel so guilty."

"I'm sorry. Why do you feel guilty?"

"Because of Mathilda. She's becoming more serious about moving here. It just so happens a couple of units are available for her and some of her convent sisters."

"And?"

"And I realized that I really don't want her to live here." Agnes looked genuinely anguished. "We've been friends for centuries. She literally saved me from starvation. How can I be so antisocial?"

"It's quite common for friends to drift apart over the years. In your case, hundreds and hundreds of years. People change, even immortal ones."

"I suppose you're right."

"And to be honest, Mathilda is a handful," I said. "She's too domineering and will upset the status quo here. In fact, it sounds like she wants to replace you as president of the HOA and nest mother."

"It's not as if I love being president. It's a lot of work and aggravation."

"But you're a truly wise and benevolent nest mother. The vampires here wouldn't appreciate an authoritarian religious ruler."

"That's for sure. Could you imagine Schwartz getting bossed around by a nun?" Agnes giggled.

"That's the solution, then." The plan unfurled in my mind like a giant blueprint. "Give her a good taste of what the vampires here are really like. The, shall we say, quirky characters."

"I don't think Mathilda will find them amusing."

"Exactly. Her instinct would be to discipline them and drive the quirkiness out of them. But they're not young women taking vows at a convent. She won't be able to change the personality of a two-hundred-year-old vampire. The residents here would rebel and drive her away."

"I think your plan has potential."

"Is Mathilda around tonight? Bring her to the creative-writing workshop. It starts in fifteen minutes."

WE'D ALREADY HEARD two readings by the time Agnes and Mathilda arrived in the community room and sat on folding chairs. Sol had read a scene from an adventure story in which he failed in his attempt to imitate Hemingway's style. Then again, Hemingway never wrote about drinking blood, so maybe it was an unfair comparison.

Doris had read a chapter from her memoir. It was Chapter 136 from a manuscript that was now more than 2,000 pages long and so far only covered the first 150 years of her existence, with another 120 to go.

Now, it was Gladys's turn. Perfect timing for the nun to arrive.

"My story is called 'Plumber's Helper,'" Gladys said as she pulled it up on her tablet. "It's an erotic romance about a lonely vampire widow whose pipes are clogged. Until a hot young shifter plumber unclogs them."

Mathilda coughed. I giggled behind my hand.

"It was three in the morning when the van pulled up at Constance's house, and a strapping young dreamboat climbed from the cab," Gladys read aloud. "He strode up her front path carrying the largest plunger Constance had ever seen."

"Oy vey," Schwartz said under his breath. "Here we go again."

"'You have such a large plunger,' Constance said, as she let him into her front door. 'It sounded like a big clog in a big pipe,' he said, fixing her with his blue eyes."

Sol hummed to himself as music leaked from his ear buds. It was a good way to block out Gladys.

"Constance showed him where her problem was, and he said he knew exactly how to fix it. He peeled the tight T-shirt from his muscular chest and—"

The cough from Mathilda was deafening. Her frowning face

was beet-red, which was quite remarkable for a deathly pale vampire. I worried about her heart.

"'The clog is severe. I need to use the snake,' he said to Constance, his chest glistening with sweat."

I looked over, and Mathilda and Agnes were gone.

Unfortunately, I had to stay for the rest of the story and its unbearable double entendres. The critiques from the group afterward were savage. Vampires make the most merciless literary critics.

But Gladys didn't take it personally. She never faltered in her passion for writing erotic romance. Nor did she ever improve at it.

AFTER THE WORKSHOP, I caught up with Agnes and Mathilda in the card room. Four vampires, particularly old in body age, were playing canasta. Agnes and Mathilda watched from a nearby table. I knew why Agnes had selected this card game to observe: these players were known to be especially competitive and unusually ornery.

The slap of cards upon the table grew louder as tensions rose within the group. Finally, it happened.

"You're cheating!" Margaret from Buffalo shouted.

"I am not, you half-blind hag!" said Alice from Detroit.

"What did you call me?"

"I called you a lousy canasta player."

"You called me a hag."

"A cheating hag!"

In a blink of an eye, the table was overturned, cards scattered like a blizzard, and the two innocent-bystander players landed on their butts on the floor.

Margaret and Alice wrestled six feet in the air, nails scratching and fangs snapping.

"A physical altercation during a card game?" Mathilda asked, aghast.

"Happens all the time with this gang," Agnes replied.

"How can you allow it to happen? You must end the fight and discipline them."

Margaret and Alice smashed into the ceiling tiles, then dropped onto the carpet. It looked as if they were attempting to pop each other's head off.

"I tried to stop them once and was seriously injured," Agnes said. "It's best to let them get it out of their systems, then all will be well."

The fight ended as suddenly as it had begun. The two elderly vampires lay on their backs on the carpet, breathing heavily. Then they broke out laughing.

"I didn't really think you were cheating," Margaret said. "I just like to get a rise out of you."

"And I don't think you're a hag. You're just a sweet, old, shriveled blood-sucking monster."

The two rolled toward each other and embraced.

"Aww," Agnes said. "All's well that ends well."

"Ridiculous," Mathilda muttered. "The vampires here are uncontrollable."

"Exactly. They like it that way."

Schwartz appeared in the doorway.

"Hey, you." He pointed at Mathilda. "Is that your hearse out there with the New York plates?"

"Yes. And don't use that tone with me."

"I've got two issues with you," he said, using the same tone. "First, why are you driving a 1960s-era hearse? You look like you came off the set of a bad horror movie."

"At the convent, we use it with a human driver to transport sisters during the daytime in their coffins."

"Second issue: you parked in my spot."

"I parked in a visitor's spot."

"Everyone here knows it's my spot. I need the closest one to the lobby door. The handicapped spots are too far away."

"Don't you have a reserved spot that comes with your unit?"

"In the parking garage." He waved his hand dismissively. "The garage reminds me of the crypt I lived in back in Brooklyn. No, thank you."

"Do I have to move my hearse?" Mathilda asked Agnes.

"You're not breaking any rules. Except his."

"I'll have you towed," Schwartz said.

"You can't do that. I'm in a visitor's spot."

"Your visitor's pass is expired. You have to get a new one each day you're here. Move your hearse or I'm calling a tow truck."

"This is absurd!" Mathilda fumed. "You need to show some respect."

"Listen, sister, I don't respect anyone who takes my parking space."

"Leonard's bark is worse than his bite," Agnes said to Mathilda. "But he's typical of the residents here."

"It's almost like you're trying to scare me away from Squid Tower."

"Nonsense. I know nothing scares you, Mathilda. Even a community as eccentric as ours."

"Eccentric? I'd call it depraved."

"This is *not* a convent." Agnes was giving her a Visigoth warrior's death stare. "We follow the rules of the HOA, not scripture. We have vampires of different faiths here and different personal ethics. You cannot impose your beliefs and morals on the residents. If you accept these unique individuals, they'll accept you."

"Rules are written in black and white. I don't believe in shades of gray."

"Perhaps, then, you wouldn't feel comfortable here."

"Can we go outside so I can enjoy the Florida weather? That's the main reason I'm here—aside from being with you, Agnes."

They left the room, and I tagged along. But as they turned into the main hall leading to the pool deck, Mathilda screamed.

Henrietta came buzzing down the hall at full speed on her mobility scooter. She narrowly missed running over Agnes and Mathilda. Close behind her came three other vampires on scooters.

"They love to race from time to time," Agnes explained. "Isn't it exciting? You need to be fast to catch prey, after all."

"Did they drink a drunkard's blood tonight?"

"No, it came from the Blood Bus. They get so energized after they feed."

After the scooters passed us, we continued down the hall and went outside. All around the pool were chaise lounges, where vampires in bathing suits soaked up the moonlight.

"You know how I feel about the immodest swimwear," Mathilda said.

"I do, indeed." Agnes scanned the ocean where someone was swimming. "Let's sit near the beach to spare your eyes the scandal of seeing uncovered flesh."

We left the pool deck and strolled along the raised wooden boardwalk that crossed over the dunes. At its end was a viewing area with benches and stairs descending to the sand.

The beach was empty in the silver moonlight. No humans would be out at this hour, and the vampires apparently preferred to be by the pool.

Only one vampire was out here: the man swimming in the ocean parallel to the beach. He had a giant beard and unruly white hair. I smiled in anticipation of what was about to happen.

Agnes waved at the swimming vampire. Eventually, she caught his eye, and he waved back.

"That's Walt Whitman, the famous American poet from the nineteenth century," Agnes said. "Have you heard of him?"

"I don't read modern poetry."

"He's quite a character. He usually attends the creative-writing workshops but wasn't there tonight. Oh, here he comes."

Walt had stopped swimming and was wading through the surf to the shore. Once the water was shallow enough, something became very apparent in the moonlight.

Walt was naked. He always swam naked.

He crossed the beach and ascended the stairs to the dune crossover, wearing nothing but a big smile.

I'd been watching Mathilda's expression, and now it registered thermonuclear rage.

"I just can't believe what you've become after you moved to Florida," she said to Agnes. "Your community is full of jerks, crazies, and perverts. It's a den of sin and a lunatic asylum."

"Welcome to Florida. Still, I think you'd fit in here."

"I wouldn't be caught undead in a place like this!"

Mathilda's footsteps pounded along the boardwalk as she fled the scene.

"Is it something I said?" Walt asked when he reached us.

"Not at all, dear," Agnes said. "You're just being your unique self. We all are. Now, wrap yourself in a towel, please."

CHAPTER 18
MAGIC HACKS

"The Friends of Cryptids Society didn't ask me to help you catch the loup-garou," Angela said when I showed up at her door the next evening.

"I know. *I'm* asking."

"Of course, I'll coordinate and assist with the extraction of the creature. But I can't actively devote my time to hunting it with you. Right now, I have several important assignments from the Society, including disciplining a Chupacabra who's gone rogue." She shivered. "Goodness, how I dread tangling with that monster."

"Yes, I understand," I said, trying to keep the fear out of my voice. "But I have serious doubts that my magic will be powerful enough to immobilize a loup-garou."

"They're really just werewolves on steroids."

"The steroids are what I'm worried about."

"Come in." She showed me to a barstool at her kitchen island. "You need a Scotch."

"You know I don't like Scotch."

"You'll acquire a taste for it."

She poured two glasses nearly full.

"Obviously," she continued, "you must capture him while he's in human form. You know he looks like his brother, so you might spot him before he sees you."

"And then he can shift at will and tear me to pieces before I can subdue him."

"Drink your Scotch and buck up, girl."

"I dropped in tonight to ask you for any help you can provide. If you don't want to help me fight it—"

"If you're in trouble, I'll come rescue you."

"Is that Plan B?"

"I beg your pardon?"

"Never mind. Can you teach me a new spell or how to strengthen my magic, so I have a better chance against him?"

I explained I would use the monster's telepathic connection with me to lure him to Furman's home or store. If I spotted him while he was in human form, no problem. But if he showed up in loup-garou form to kill Furman, I'd be at a disadvantage.

"Also," I said, "I don't want him to show up and kill Furman when I'm not there. I don't want him to kill Furman at all, frankly. I feel like I already have the blood of three werewolves on my hands."

"Nonsense. The murders weren't your fault. First, I'll teach you how to make an amulet that will alert you when he's trying to read your mind and give you an idea of his location. Be careful, though. Avoid thinking about capturing him. You don't want to tip him off to your plans. With the spell, you might also be able to recall his unique psychic energy, which would help you locate him, even when he's not telepathically connected to you."

Angela explained she had developed the innate ability to detect someone else's telepathy. I could do so, too, but it would take several months of training. Wearing the amulet would give me the ability instantly. She consulted a grimoire that was on a shelf next to cookbooks and wrote the ingredients for the amulet and instructions for the spell to activate it.

"The other magic hack I'll teach you will require that talisman you have."

"The Red Dragon?"

"Yes. Naturally, you'll want to always have it with you until you capture the loup-garou, so it can strengthen your sleep and immobility spells. Do you know any calming spells?"

"Yeah. I have one I use on myself increasingly often."

"Good. Hold the Red Dragon while you're casting the spell. And include the words, *'non mutare manent absolutem.'* And it will slow or halt his shifting process. It's like throwing a wrench in the gears."

"Really? That's incredible."

"Yeah. With effort, he'll be able to overcome the effects of the spell, but it will give you time to subdue him with other spells while he's still fully or partially human."

"Thank you."

"Do you feel better now?" Angela asked.

"A little. Could be the Scotch, though."

"You're a formidable witch, Missy. You will prevail."

As soon as I got home, I worked on making the amulet. The good thing about managing witchcraft supplies at the Jellyfish Beach Mystical Mart & Botanica was I always had almost every conceivable ingredient on hand in my garage workroom. From obscure roots and herbs to disgusting bits of previously living creatures, I had them all. Or I could order them with overnight shipping.

Using a mortar and pestle, plus my mini food processor, I combined all the ingredients and filled a small felt sack with them. Next, I performed the spell using Angela's notes and enchanted the amulet.

I attached the sack to a leather cord and hung it around my neck. And almost immediately, I sensed the loup-garou probing me.

He was on the edge of my property, not close enough to set off the wards. I cleared my mind of all thoughts, which wasn't easy, but I had a lot of practice doing so when spell-casting.

Then, I thought about Fred Furman. I pictured him in his store, not his home, because he'd probably be safer in his store. I thought about how he was the president of the Downtown Merchants Association. It wasn't so much a leadership position as a business-administrative one, but he was the closest thing to an alpha they had—until Dunott came along.

I concentrated on his role in pushing back against Dunott's harassment. Though, as a werewolf, Furman couldn't have fired the silver bullets, he could have ordered it done. And he most likely had the funding to hire better hitmen than Maddie had.

Again, I kept my focus on Furman in his store. I replayed memories of visiting him there and my plans to visit him again for further questions. I forced myself to feel confident that he was our prime suspect.

Suddenly, a weight fell from my mind as the loup-garou's telepathic connection ceased. I had the strong feeling he had left the area, as well.

Hopefully, this ruse had worked. I would find out soon enough.

MATT and I were waiting outside Furman's boutique the next morning when he unlocked the front door and reversed the sign hanging on it to "open."

"Something tells me you're not here to buy catnip," Furman said, opening the door.

"No, I'm here because I can't get that platinum paper-weight off my mind," I replied.

"What do you want?" He remained standing in the door-way, blocking our passage.

"We have a few more questions for you," Matt said.

"I got nothing else to say to you people."

"You should let us in," I said. "We have information you'll want to hear."

He grunted and stepped away, letting the door swing into my face. We followed him to the main counter.

"What is it?"

"The police consider you the prime suspect in Dunott's murder," I said. It wasn't exactly a lie because the police prob-ably suspected him. To some degree, at least.

"That's ridiculous. There's a loup-garou out there murdering werewolves like me. He probably did it."

"Dunott was killed with silver bullets before the fire was set."

Furman stared back at me impassively. His face wasn't giving anything away.

"We think a killer-for-hire did it," Matt said. "After previous hired killers failed."

"What does that have to do with me?"

"We think you hired the killer."

Furman laughed. Actually, it was more of a growl.

"I've said before that we were going to take down Dunott through litigation."

"And it was going nowhere."

"I wouldn't know how to hire a hitman."

"If you have the money, you could have found a way."

"You've got no proof. You're just bluffing."

"We have enough proof to make you our prime suspect," I said. "Unless you have information that points to someone else. Now is not the time to take a fall to protect them."

My senses alerted me we were about to be interrupted. No, it wasn't the amulet doing it. It was my built-in butthead detector.

The front door opened, and two men walked in. I recognized them, and neither was Dunott's brother.

It was Timothy Tissy, aka Lord Arseton of the Knights Simplar. With him was the tall, stooped guy I had seen walking his dog near the park where the werewolves were meeting. They weren't attired in ridiculous Renaissance-style garb today. It would be hard for Furman to take them seriously if they were. They had a different uniform of sorts: jeans and black hoodies.

"Can I help you, gentlemen?" Furman asked.

"We were wondering if we could help *you*," Lord Arseton said.

"I only buy from my regular suppliers."

"I'm talking about helping you move out of Jellyfish Beach."

"Are you crazy?"

"We know all about you," Arseton said menacingly. "Your secret alternate identity."

"I don't know what you're talking about."

"Yes, you do. Think of howling at the full moon."

"Are you on drugs? Get out of my store or I'm calling the police."

"We are the Knights Simplar, a secret holy order that is dedicated to ridding the world of Satanic creatures like yourself. We will show you mercy and allow you to move away from this town. If you don't, we will put you down like a sick dog."

Furman pulled a pistol from beneath the counter and laid it on the glass countertop.

"I've had a lot of experience being harassed by thugs," he said. "The last one is now resting in his grave."

Arseton laughed. He meant to do it with bravado, but it sounded kind of nervous to me.

"There are other werewolves in this town," he said. "It would be a shame to burn you all at the stake. Or maybe we'll just burn down your store."

"You're on security cameras right now, moron. With audio. I think you should reconsider your threats."

"Freedom of speech, you spawn of Satan."

Arseton and his accomplice swaggered up to the counter, ignoring the gun on it.

"And there are two witnesses," I said.

"Mind your own business, witch," Arseton said. "The only thing keeping you alive is being the daughter of Saint Ruth. Until she decides that you shall die."

Yes, I thought, we mustn't forget about the other aggravations in my life.

"Timmy, you're in way over your head here," I said. "I suggest you leave this man alone."

"We will for now." He sauntered toward the door, his goon right behind him. "But we'll be back. And we'll be breaking things."

After they finally left, Furman turned to me.

"You know them?"

"Yes. And they're correct in that they fancy themselves as the enemies of supernaturals. They're incompetent, but unfortunately, they have learned that werewolves exist. So, I'd keep an eye on them if I were you."

"Now I have to worry about them as well as the loup-garou?"

"We hope the latter will be taken care of," I said. "And these guys, too. Eventually. But let's get back to our previous discussion."

"I don't have any information for you. I had nothing to do with killing Dunott and don't know who did it."

"You werewolves had a great motive to get rid of him. Who else would?"

"Why are you asking me? You two have been bothering

everyone in town with your questions. You would know better than I who had a motive."

"Do me a favor, and ask around."

"I'm doing you no favors."

He wasn't going to tell us more, so we would have to return to bother him again.

CHAPTER 19

THE ENEMY OF MY ENEMY

The following evening, I was enjoying quiet time after dinner, with a mystery novel and a cup of tea, sitting in my easy chair with the cats curled up beside the ottoman. Tony was asleep in the garage, so I wasn't pestered by someone talking or trying to connect with me telepathically.

Until someone was. The magic in my amulet alerted me that Dunott's brother was, once again, reading my mind.

I switched my train of thought to center on Furman, our visit with him at his shop, and his denials under questioning. I had been genuinely skeptical of his innocence. He probably didn't murder Dunott himself, but I believed he might have been involved in hiring a killer. At the very least, he probably knew who killed Dunott.

All these thoughts filled my mind, and the loup-garou fed upon them. But this time, I followed Angela's instructions and studied the monster's psychic energy, hoping to track him.

When my mind was freed of the telepathic probing, I attempted to remain connected with him. It wasn't easy, even with the Red Dragon in my hand.

Quickly, I cast a simplified version of my locator spell. I didn't have a possession of Dunott's brother's from which to harvest his psychic energy. All I had was the tenuous telepathic connection enabled by my amulet.

With these two magical powers, I sensed Dunott's brother leaving my neighborhood. My connection was growing weaker with distance, so I took a gamble. I got in my car and headed in his direction.

Smart, Missy. Here I was, wearing just a T-shirt, sweat-pants, and flip-flops, armed with nothing but the Red Dragon and my magic, driving blindly into the night in search of a monster.

I couldn't tell which street my quarry was taking, but I knew he was traveling north, toward downtown, and I was quickly gaining on him. He must be on foot. I hoped they were human feet right now, not those of a loup-garou.

Headlights filled my rearview mirror from an impatient driver. Checking my speed, I realized I was only going twenty-five miles an hour. Too fast for a human to sustain on foot. Could the monster be riding a bicycle? No, that didn't seem like a monster kind of thing to do.

He must have shifted into wolf form.

I called Matt and told him what I was doing.

"Are you crazy?" he said. "Don't you dare confront the monster until I get there."

"How are you going to help me?"

"I have silver bullets now, remember?"

"I'm supposed to capture, not kill it."

"I want to make sure you don't get killed. I'm on my way now."

My psychic connection to the monster grew stronger. I didn't see him ahead of me, so he must be moving parallel to me. I turned right, traveled one block, and turned left.

An enormous wolf trotted along the street at a comfortable pace.

It was approaching 10:00 p.m., and my town of mostly retirees was pretty much shut down for the night. But it was risky for Dunott's brother to travel in wolf form. A few businesses were still open, and someone might come upon him. There weren't wolves in Florida anymore, particularly not wolves this big. If he were spotted, it would cause a public outcry.

The creature turned his head and saw me, then turned away. He didn't care that a car was behind him. Obviously, he didn't realize I was tracking his psychic energy. His attention was completely focused on his hunt.

We reached the boulevard. Furman's boutique, on the corner, had its lights blazing. Why was he still open at this hour?

I parked my car in an alley and approached the store on foot. The wolf was nowhere to be seen. I had promised Matt I wouldn't do anything until he arrived, but I had a bad feeling about this.

The store's closed sign showed in the glass door. A man inside walked past it, and he wasn't Furman. In fact, he was wearing a black hoodie.

I crept to a side window and peeked through it. The situation in there did not look good.

Fred Furman, in human form, sat in a chair next to a wall display. Arseton, the stooped guy, and a third member of the Knights Simplar stood over him. Arseton pointed a handgun at Furman. I cast a spell to enhance my hearing and pick up what they were saying.

"This is the last time I'm going to tell you," Arseton said to Furman. "Write down the names of every werewolf who owns a business in Jellyfish Beach."

"I don't know every name."

"Don't play stupid with me!"

Arseton spat in Furman's face. He leered at the old man, waiting to see what he would do.

Slowly, feebly, Fred pulled a tissue from his pocket. He weakly dabbed his face dry and dropped the tissue.

It was only then that I noticed the delicate silver chain of a necklace draped over one of his shoulders. The silver was making him weak and helpless.

Arseton pressed the muzzle of the gun into Furman's neck, causing him to scream in agony. Thin wisps of smoke rose from his burned flesh. The gun obviously was loaded with silver bullets.

Furman's suffering made Arseton laugh and look at his associates with delight.

"These bullets are the real thing!" he said to them.

"We should just kill him now and find the other werewolves on our own," said the stooped goon. "Can't be that hard, now that we know where in town to look."

"Freddie here is going to tell us. Aren't you, Freddie?"

Arseton leered sadistically as he pressed the gun to Furman's skin again, causing another scream.

"Let's get this over with," said the third goon, who was blond, bearded, and reminded me of a Viking. Any guesses at what kind of historical garb he wears when the Knights Simplar attend Renaissance festivals?

I would never find out, because the front door shattered, and the giant wolf leaped through the broken glass and grabbed the third goon in his jaws.

Arseton turned to shoot the wolf, but the creature's momentum pushed the goon he was chewing on into Arseton, knocking him off balance.

The gun fired, extinguishing a fluorescent light on the ceiling.

When Arseton fell over, his body flipped Furman and the chair he was in backward. The chair hit the floor, and the silver chain was jolted off Furman's body.

Freed from the enervating effect of the silver, Furman jumped to his feet and shifted into a wolf. A smaller one than the loup-garou. With jaws snapping, he went right for Arseton's face.

Meanwhile, I was busily casting a sleep spell, which I directed with a wide radius into the room, hoping to affect everyone inside before all the humans were dead.

I should say, the remaining humans. It was too late for the Viking.

Arseton and the stooped guy staggered and slowly eased themselves to the floor, where they slumped over, snoring. Furman whimpered, then curled up on the carpet. While asleep, he involuntarily shifted back to human.

The loup-garou was unaffected by my spell. His head moved back and forth, sniffing the air, as if he could locate the source of the spell that way.

He could. His head swiveled toward the window I was hiding beside.

I ran for my car in the nearby alley and was yanking the door open when the loup-garou sped after me. I closed and locked the door, before he reached my car, and cast the fastest version of a protection spell I could manage.

Except now, he was in half-human form. He was still covered in the black wolf fur, but he stood upright, and his body had human proportions. His fingers and toes ended in long, sharp, curved nails, and his head was that of a wolf.

His head was the truly jarring sight that sent tingling down my spine and nausea through my stomach. It was larger than a human head, and his dark, yellow-rimmed eyes looked at me with eerie intelligence above a long muzzle. Saliva dripped from his mouth.

Though he walked on two legs like a human, his steps had a springier action than ours do. His pace was slow and deliberate, as if he had all the time in the world. Even when I started the engine, he seemed in no rush.

I had parked in the alley front-first, so the loup-garou was approaching the rear of my car. Further down the alley, my headlights hit a dumpster that blocked any passage. I would have to back up to get out of here.

When he entered the alley, I put the car in reverse and floored it. Not that my ancient Toyota four-cylinder had a lot of oomph, but it rocketed backward.

The impact when it slammed into the loup-garou made my

head snap forward. The car was still, as if I had hit a wall, the tires spinning uselessly on the asphalt.

The creature stood behind my trunk and bent down. My car's rear end lifted. The front-wheel drivetrain strained from the additional weight on the front tires, which still could not propel the car and were burning rubber. I took my foot off the gas.

This thing was way too strong. My only hope for survival was to snap out of my panic and cast my immobility spell, my sleep spell having proved to be useless against the loup-garou.

Clutching the Red Dragon in my left hand, I concentrated on gathering my energies and drawing power from the talisman to enhance them. The problem was, concentrating was almost impossible.

I was feeling the warmth building in my solar plexus when the monster released my rear bumper, and the car landed hard, jolting me out of my focus.

I tried again as the creature walked around my car, his toenails clicking on the asphalt. He approached my door. My heart returned to rattling like a jackhammer. The immobility spell was not going to happen.

The loup-garou grabbed the handle of my locked door and tugged, making the car shake from side to side. I strengthened my protection spell. It was too late to put up the bubble around the entire car because the creature had already made contact with it. I would have to be content with protecting just myself.

The monster yanked at the door handle again to the sound of straining metal. I remembered all too well seeing Leticia's car with its door torn off.

Without thinking, I tried to push him away from the car

with my telekinesis. He leaned backward and paused briefly before continuing to pull at my door. Angela was right: my telekinesis only worked with inanimate objects or willing creatures such as Percy.

Why did Matt have a gun with silver bullets and not me? Probably because, in my arrogance, I believed magic would protect me and that firearms were for normal humans.

The monster pulled again, and with a loud bang, the door popped off. I screamed.

Screams wouldn't protect me, but maybe noise would help. I sent a burst of energy that set off the car alarm. My car's lights flashed, and the horn beeped rhythmically as the monster reached inside the car for me. I leaned away, almost frozen in fear.

His hairy hands with their needle nails stopped when they hit the protection bubble. But he didn't appear willing to give up.

I pumped more magic into my car's electrical system, increasing the volume of the alarm. The loup-garou covered his ears with his hands. This noise must be painful to his super-sensitive hearing.

That didn't change the fact that I was stuck in my car. The monster couldn't get his teeth and nails into me as long as my spell held up, but he could prevent me from escaping. And if he tried hard enough, his preternatural strength might eventually breach my bubble.

A gunshot rang out behind me, and a piece of shattered brick flew from the building beside my car, landing on the windshield.

The loup-garou stood straight, withdrawing from my open door. His nostrils flared, taking in scents.

Then he took off. I caught a glimpse of him as he leaped over the dumpster further down the alley before he was gone.

Matt appeared beside my car.

"Are you trying to turn your car into an open-air dune buggy?" he asked.

"I'm in no mood for jokes right now."

"Sorry I'm such a lousy shot, but at least it scared him away. Now we're down to only three silver bullets."

"We can get more."

"I saw the door to Furman's shop was busted open. I was about to go inside when I heard the car alarm. When it doubled in volume, I knew you had something to do with it."

"We had enemies versus enemies going on in there," I explained. "The Knights Simplar were holding Furman against his will, threatening to shoot him with silver bullets if he didn't give them a list of all the werewolves in town. That's when the loup-garou showed up. I think he came to attack Furman, but Arseton's goons got in his way."

I told him how my sleep spell had neutralized everyone except the loup-garou. And I mentioned that Furman was so sensitive to silver that the gun had burned his skin because of the bullets inside the gun.

After I released my protection spell, we left the alley and walked to Furman's boutique.

"I don't know why I hadn't suspected the Knights Simplar of Dunott's murder until now," I said. "It makes sense. They've said they want to kill werewolves, and they have silver bullets." I smacked my forehead with my palm. "Why was I so stupid?"

"Because the local merchants had such a strong, urgent motive. And the Knights Simplar are a bunch of morons. I don't believe they've ever killed a quote-unquote monster."

"Dunott may have been the first. I'm going to use my truth-telling spell on Arseton to find out."

When we went inside Furman's store, I was shocked to find everyone gone except for Furman. His jowly face was pale and looked shocked by what he had gone through. He had put the clothes back on that had fallen off when he shifted earlier, even though the seams had burst in many places.

Round, red burn marks stood out on his neck where the pistol had touched him.

"Did you use some witchy magic to make us fall asleep?" Furman asked me.

"Yes. And it shouldn't have worn off so quickly. I was going to interrogate the men who assaulted you."

"They were already gone when I woke up. They took the body of their buddy with them, but as you can see, there's a lot of blood to clean up. I'm going to report this as an attempted robbery, but I think I'll leave out the part about the dead guy. I want these jerks arrested."

"I'm afraid they're going to be a major headache to you guys unless we stop them."

"Do you think they murdered Dunott?" Furman asked.

"I do now."

As Matt and I were leaving the store, taking care not to step in any blood, I noticed a crumpled tissue on the floor. It was the one Furman had used to wipe off Arseton's spittle. I took it, realizing it might come in handy for tracking our new prime suspect. As a nurse, I was accustomed to handling disgusting things.

I told Matt I would need his help the next day.

"We're going to go to Arseton's workplace to solve this mystery once and for all. And you're driving because I'm missing a door."

CHAPTER 20

GUARD DEMON

The next day, Matt drove me to Lord Arseton's workplace. Matt couldn't go inside with me, because he had a little history with Arseton; namely, Matt had infiltrated the Knights Simplar, and they tried to kill him for it.

Lord Arseton worked at a place that didn't fit his imaginary lordship status. I should use his real name, Tim Tissy, manager of You Break It, We Try to Fix It. Yes, his lordship repaired broken smartphones.

We parked outside the store, which was in a small shopping plaza, and waited until after dark when it was nearly closing time and no customers were inside. I sauntered through the door. A pimply faced young man was behind the counter.

"Can I help you?" he asked.

"I need to speak with the manager. He's helped me with my phone before and knows the exact issue."

"Um, yeah, okay." He went into the back room.

Arseton appeared and frowned when he saw me.

"I have an issue with my phone that only you can solve," I said.

He looked very wary of me. Who could blame him?

"Please let me show you," I said in my friendliest voice. I needed him to come to the counter opposite me, so I could reach over it while showing him my screen and surreptitiously sprinkle the magical powder on his feet.

"You don't really have a problem with your phone, do you?"

"Why else would I be here?"

My spell was all cued up to go if he would only get close enough to me.

"I dropped my phone," I said, "and now it's not responding."

He moved a little closer, but still was too far away.

"Your phone looks fine."

"The touchscreen isn't working right. See for yourself."

He shook his head and looked rather nervous for a self-professed lord who fought the minions of Satan.

Realizing he wasn't falling for my ruse, I got more direct.

"You were at The Cat's Meow last night," I said. "You threatened to kill Fred Furman."

"No, I wasn't."

"I saw you through a window."

"Impossible," he said, looking very scared right now.

"One of your men was mauled by a wolf."

Arseton shook his head. "I'm sorry, but I can't help you. I'm asking you to leave now before I call the police."

"I'll be talking to you soon, Timmy."

I walked out, frustrated. It was time to alter my plans.

"You don't look happy," Matt said, leaning against his truck, facing the store. "It looked like he didn't get close enough to the counter."

"He didn't. We're going to try something more physical."

"You want me to tackle him and hold him down?"

"No. I'm going to use my immobility spell on him."

I recognized Arseton's car parked in a distant part of the lot where, fortunately, the lighting was poor. Matt followed my gaze and seemed to read my mind. We both got in the truck, and he positioned us close, but not too close. We slumped in our seats so he wouldn't see us and waited until we saw him lock the store for the night and head toward his car.

I went through the ritual and cast the spell. Arseton froze in mid-stride like a statue, and I jumped out of the car, standing in front of him as if we were having a real conversation in case anyone saw us.

The conversation was far from real, because under my immobility spell, the only thing allowing him to speak was my truth spell, which I cast as I sprinkled the powder on him.

"What did you do with the body of your friend who was killed last night?" I asked.

"We brought him to the landfill," he replied quite eagerly. "There are ghouls who scavenge there who will dispose of him."

"Do you know what killed him?"

"It was an abnormally powerful werewolf. So powerful it wasn't afraid of us."

"Okay. Have you killed any werewolves?"

"Not any in wolf form."

"Did you kill Pierre Dunott? Tell the truth."

"I don't know who he is."

"The city commissioner—"

We were no longer alone. A giant eye floated in the air between us.

It was Myron, the cacodemon who Arseton believed was an angel. Now that the Knights Simplar served my mother, she had used her black magic to bind the demon to her, as well.

"Get out of my face, Myron," I said unwisely.

The giant floating eyeball shot a bolt of lightning at me, knocking me on my butt. My derrière ached, but I didn't receive any burns from the bolt.

"Myron," I said, "Lord Arseton and I were just having a little talk."

This time, I rolled away before the bolt hit me. Instead, it set a discarded soda cup on fire. I cast a protection spell around myself.

I had battled Myron once before, but Angela had been with me, and it took our combined powers to defeat the demon. It would be impossible for me to beat him tonight, but with my protection bubble around me, he couldn't beat me, either. We would have to call it a draw.

"Okay," I said, getting back on my feet. "I will break my spell on Lord Arseton. I will get in my friend's truck, and we'll leave. That will be the end of it tonight."

The giant eyeball had no way of answering me. It only hovered there above my head, waiting for me to fulfill my promise.

I uttered the words and snapped my fingers, releasing both spells.

"What did you do to me?" Arseton asked me.

"Nothing."

"Myron wouldn't have come unless I was in trouble."

"Everything's okay now. I'll be talking to you soon."

I got in Matt's truck, and we drove slowly away, watching Myron hover above Arseton as he got into his car. The giant eyeball rose into the night sky and disappeared.

"That demon really freaks me out," Matt said. "How could those nuts believe he's an angel?"

"There are many evil things in the world that people convince themselves are good because doing so validates their worldview. Or, to put it simply, the Knights Simplar are a bunch of fools."

And I would need to make those fools confess to Dunott's murder.

WE FOLLOWED Arseton to the apartment complex where he lived. I hoped to ambush him again with my immobility and truth spells. Matt turned off his headlights as we followed him through the entrance and parked a safe distance from his space.

He got out of his car and started walking toward the stairs. It was showtime.

But just as I was opening my door to catch up with him, Myron appeared above me.

"He's going to zap you again," Matt said.

I closed my door. "Arseton's guard demon is making my life difficult. Let's see if Arseton is going out tonight. Maybe I'll get an opportunity to catch him without Myron."

We left the apartment complex but parked next to a nearby grocery store right across the street. From here, I could see Arseton's building and the stairs. That is, I could see with a spell that enhanced my distance vision for those inconvenient moments when you don't have binoculars handy.

I didn't have to wait long before I saw him walking down the stairs carrying a garment bag. I knew, from a previous stakeout, that the bag contained a tunic Arseton wore for his regular ceremonies with his followers. And I knew the chain hotel where he held them.

I told Matt what I had seen.

"Oh, no. I don't want to go to that hotel again."

"You had a traumatic experience last time. But you're not trying to infiltrate the group tonight. You're just going to sit safely in your truck while I spy on them. I'm hoping to hear something that will incriminate them."

"That stupid demon will be there."

"That's okay. I'll stay away from Arseton."

"I don't have a good feeling about this."

"Don't be such a Negative Nelly, Matt. I'm just spying."

So, there I was again, on the north side of the hotel, pressing my hands against the exterior concrete wall, using my penetration spell to burrow, metaphorically, through the wall and observe what was going on in the meeting room on the other side.

In the past, I'd had great success using the penetration spell on this very same wall. So, I'd decided not to use the tissue with Arseton's spittle to cast the altered version of the spell I had used with Maddie and Furman. I wanted to save his psychic energy in case I needed to use the altered version later.

The original penetration spell was effective, but it required I touch the wall of the building. Which had its downsides.

A man wandered by through the parking lot.

"Are you holding up the wall or are you as drunk as I am?" he asked. "Getting the head spins is awful."

I ignored him and resumed my spell. Soon, voices from inside the meeting room came to me. Next, images appeared in my head, blurry at first, but coming into focus. I now had a full connection to the room.

And what I saw surprised me.

It was unlike previous meetings I had observed, which had been people holding hands in a circle taking part in a combination of a religious service and angry rants by Arseton. Tonight, they sat in rows of folding chairs facing a speaker standing before them.

My mother.

Arseton stood behind her, and kneeling on the floor in front of her was poor Fred Furman. I could see a thin silver chain around his neck incapacitating him. The poor guy just couldn't catch a break.

"You werewolves thought you could dominate the downtown business district," Ruth Bent said to Furman, "and no one would find out that you're werewolves?"

"Yes," Furman replied in a weak voice. "It worked for years."

"Not anymore. Now werewolves are being murdered one after another, right?"

Furman could barely move his head to nod.

"You didn't kill them, did you?" Ruth asked Arseton.

"No, Saint Ruth."

"Have you ever killed a werewolf?"

"No, your holiness. We almost killed one last night, but another werewolf attacked us."

"It was a loup-garou," Furman said. "A rare and especially powerful kind of werewolf. He's the one who has been killing members of our pack."

"Ah, I see. You don't need to worry any longer. I had you brought here tonight to propose an offer. I will protect your pack if you join my coven."

"We're not witches," Furman said.

"It doesn't matter. Call it a temple instead of a coven, then. All that matters is that your pack follows me."

"How so? What do we have to do?"

"You need to worship me, of course. But who wouldn't want to do that? You also will serve as security for me from time to time. Most important, you must pay monthly dues. Plus, give me generous discounts at your establishments."

Furman was angry, even in his weakened state.

"We don't want to be shaken down again. That's what Commissioner Dunott did to us."

"Is he the commissioner who was murdered?"

"Yes."

"By you guys?"

"We don't know who killed him."

"What about you, Lord Arseton?"

"I don't know, your holiness. Neither I nor any of my men did it, I am certain."

"Wasn't he murdered because he was taking payments from your pack?" Ruth asked Furman.

"I don't know. And he was shaking down all the businesses, by the way, not just the ones owned by my pack."

"Well, then. He's gone, and I'm here. I'll take up where he left off, which shouldn't be a problem for you guys. You must have already budgeted for his protection-money payments. Mine are due at the first of the month. With penalties if you're late."

Furman hung his head. Probably in despair, but the silver wasn't helping, either.

"From this moment forward, no one will harass the werewolves of Jellyfish Beach. Except for me. You hear that, Arseton? No intimidation and no killing."

"What about the loup-garou?" Furman asked. "Will you protect us from him?"

"Yes, I will. That's included in the dues you pay me."

I doubted she knew how dangerous loup-garous were.

"Now, let this werewolf go," she commanded, "and we will begin the ceremony of worshipping me—Saint Ruth, the kind, the merciful, and the almighty . . . What is that?"

The Knights Simplar looked at her in confusion. Furman, freed of the silver chain, staggered from the room.

"I detect magic. Hostile magic. It's intruding into this room."

Uh-oh. I went through the steps of releasing the spell, which were not simple, my energy and consciousness having extended themselves through stucco, concrete block, and drywall.

My head exploded in sharp pain, and my vision went black. A force clenched my throat until I couldn't breathe.

I tried to push myself away from the building, but it was as if I were still in the meeting room.

And I couldn't get out.

CHAPTER 21

BALLPOINT PENITENTIARY

The energy that tethered my consciousness to my body was suddenly severed. My mind, my identity, my memories—everything that made me who I am —was taken. The last thing I remembered about my body was the feeling of my palms against the rough texture of the stucco on the hotel wall and the steady rumbling of traffic on the nearby interstate.

Now, my body was merely an empty husk. It was still alive, but I just wasn't inside it.

Instead, I was in a hell of my mother's making.

"You were spying on me!" her voice rang out. I heard it, though I no longer had ears. The audio was probably coming to me through her ears.

No, I wasn't, I replied in thought, though not in my actual voice. *I was spying on the Knights Simplar and didn't know you'd be here.*

"You were using your magic against me, instead of for me.

It's one thing to not want to join my coven. But to work actively against me is unacceptable."

This has nothing to do with you.

"Everything is about me."

You're such a narcissist.

"Yes. I love the only one in this world worth loving. Me."

What have you done to me? Let me go now!

"I've put you in captivity."

But where?

"You're inside a ballpoint pen. The hotel put a bunch of free pens in this meeting room. I love free stuff."

My consciousness is trapped inside a pen that says "Harmony Inn Express" on it?

"Yes. You are now a cheap pen that I will lose among the clutter of my purse, or someone will accidentally take it from me. That's what you get for defying me."

I heard voices behind her. The meeting must still be going on. The voices came together in a song, kind of like a Gregorian chant. I caught the words, "Saint Ruth, the all-powerful."

This was too much. Though my physical brain, its neurons and synapses were still in my head outside the hotel, I feared I would go insane.

Suddenly, I felt dizzy, as if I were being jerked and jostled. I realized Ruth was using me to take notes.

After the chanting ended, she told everyone in the room that she had an announcement to make.

"From now on, I shall no longer be known as Saint Ruth. I shall be Saint Ruthless."

The Knights Simplar gasped in wonderment, then applauded.

It was a fitting name for the woman who had tried to kill me in the past and now held me prisoner in a ballpoint pen.

From the background noise, it sounded like the meeting was breaking up. Or, I should say, the ceremony of worship had come to its conclusion.

"Go spread the word to the business owners of Jellyfish Beach," she commanded the Knights Simplar. "I am the new, improved version of their corrupt commissioner. And I expect my dues to be paid on time."

I heard no more sounds as I was tossed into a purse among other pens, a pack of cigarettes, a wallet, a makeup kit, and a half-eaten donut.

This was not good. Cut off from my body's internal energies, I didn't know how I'd be able to use my magic. And magic was the only way I could escape from the Harmony Inn Express pen that still had its cap on.

TECHNICALLY, I wasn't dead. Not yet, at least. So, I wasn't a disembodied soul. The closest comparison I could think of was a genie trapped in a bottle. Did I have access to the spirit world? Or was the ballpoint pen a prison cell in solitary confinement?

I tried to not sink into the deepest despair. Never before had I felt so helpless and isolated. And this was on top of being nowhere near solving Dunott's murder, my most likely suspects having been ruled out.

My darkest days as an intensive care nurse had been brighter than this. My most impoverished nights working as a home-health nurse for vampires and werewolves were cheerier than this.

Why had I signed on to the mission of the Friends of Cryptids? Their huge influx of cash had turned my life around, but not in the way I had hoped.

Then, there was my mother, who had once again put my life in peril. It wasn't my fault I was born to an evil person, but once I had learned about her, and met her, why hadn't I stayed miles away?

Her demand that I join her coven was also not my fault. Yet I doubt she would have opened a Jellyfish Beach location for her coven if I hadn't lived here.

Feeling sorry for myself wasn't going to help me, I realized.

Is anybody out there? I called out. *Don Mateo, can you hear me?*

Don Mateo was bound to me through the grimoire he once owned that I kept in my house. I had my doubts that he could hear me. Still, I kept trying to reach him.

Don Mateo, I need your help. I'm not in my body, but I'm still on the physical plane, trapped inside a pen.

M'lady, is that really you? his Spanish-accented voice asked.

Yes, it's me!

It is only because of my close connection to you that I was able to hear you. As you said, you are still in the physical realm, yet I heard you here in the spirit world. How may I assist you?

I was performing a penetration spell, which enabled my consciousness to go through walls to observe a meeting. My mother, the evil sorceress, captured my consciousness and detached it from my body.

I sensed dismay in him. *Ouch! That is not good.*

Is there a way I can use my magic to escape?

As you know, I was once a powerful wizard, but as a ghost, I can no longer create magic. I would think the same would be true for you.

No offense, but you died. Your physical body is long gone. But my body is still alive; I'm just not connected to it. Is there any way I can access the natural magic my body contains?

If I were still Missy, and he were visiting me as an apparition, he would be frowning and shaking his head right now.

Madam, I don't know how. You have been imprisoned by black magic.

There must be a way. And that way might be Don Mateo himself. Yes, I was held inside this pen against my will. But Don Mateo could go anywhere he wanted. Being tied to the grimoire gave him an easy entry into the physical world and made him more inclined to haunt my house, but he wasn't limited to it.

I explained my reasoning to him.

You want me to visit your body, take some of your magical energy, and bring it to you inside the sorceress's satchel? he asked.

Purse. And yes, you're correct.

But how do I take the energy? I am merely a ghost.

Ghosts hold energy, I said. *That's how your apparition appears in the physical world.*

But it is only mild energy.

It's enough to manipulate the panties you steal from my drawer. And I'm sure you can carry even more energy than that. I only need a little. I won't be casting a spell to move mass in the physical world or stuff like that. Just enough energy to escape this stupid ballpoint pen.

He pushed back, saying I would need enough power to overcome the sorceress's magic.

I don't believe she needed that much to imprison me, I said. *My consciousness was already extended out from my body when she captured it.*

So be it, m'lady. I will make the attempt.

I told him where to look for my body. My guess was that mother and her purse were still on the hotel property, so Don Mateo wouldn't have to go far to find me.

Minutes later—or, who knows, it could have been hours—Don Mateo returned.

I cannot find your body, m'lady.

What?

It was not where you told me to look, nor anywhere outside the hotel.

Dang. Someone must have found it and taken it away. There's nothing creepier than having your body go missing when you're still alive.

The best scenario was that Matt found me and realized I was completely unresponsive. The worst was that some stranger discovered a comatose woman propped up against the hotel wall, and I was taken by an ambulance.

Do you know what Matt's truck looks like? I asked Don Mateo. *Look for it in the hotel parking lot. I'm hoping Matt put my body in it and hasn't left the property yet.*

Is it red?

You could call it red, minus years of sun bleaching and with a touch of rust.

This was turning into even more of a nightmare. I could be

trapped in the pen forever until my ink dries up, and I spend eternity in the back of a drawer or in a landfill.

The purse I was in shook violently, and I sensed a hand rummaging through its contents. The hand grabbed me and pulled me out into the open.

"Is that you?" Ruth asked. "I seem to have stolen more than one Harmony Inn Express pen."

It's me. Can you let me go free now?

"The offer was, you join my coven or die. You haven't joined. So, if I free you from the pen, I'll just have to kill you."

I haven't reached my deadline yet.

"You're very close to it. I gave you a vision of what your life could be like with the power of black magic. You could use it to heal incurable diseases and be a saint." She cackled. "A goody-two-shoes kind of saint, unlike me."

Yes, your vision was very enticing, but I haven't decided yet. Your magic is so different from mine. It would be such a difficult change. I've built a life for myself and don't want to give it up.

"Listen, dearie. I showed you one scenario of a life with black magic. But you can take other paths. You don't have to give up your silly little elemental magic. The black magic will simply enhance it. You can continue working in that dumpy bodega—"

Botanica.

"Whatever. You can do whatever you want with your black magic if you join my coven, pay my dues, and obey my every command."

Um, you're not being very persuasive.

I sensed anger. Even trapped in a cheap plastic ballpoint pen, I could tell I had poked the bear.

"I'm going to snap you in half and throw you away!"

Please don't, almighty Saint Ruthless.

She cackled. "Oh, I do love the sound of that."

Give me a little more time to consider your offer. I am so close to saying yes.

"Don't jerk me around!"

I'm being sincere, I said with my best fake sincerity.

"I think, perhaps, I will put your spirit into a little dog. A cockapoo or something. I'll make you lick my face, and I'll kick you when you pee inside the house."

Saint Ruthless, I'm curious how you'll protect the werewolves from the loup-garou? I asked, trying to stall while Don Mateo looked for my body.

"Oh, I haven't made any plans yet. I could set booby-wards at their businesses and homes. In black magic, our wards can be lethal when they're activated."

Brilliant!

"Why is the loup-garou attacking them, anyway?"

For revenge. He's the brother of the commissioner who was murdered. He must assume one of the werewolves did it but can't figure out which one. Which hasn't stopped him from killing everybody we suspect.

"He only needs to come to me. For the right price, I'll hex his enemies."

I think he enjoys mauling them to death.

Just then, I sensed Don Mateo had returned.

I found your body, he said. *Your friend, Matt, was about to take it to the hospital. I materialized in his vehicle and scared him nearly to death, before convincing him to move it near the one you're inside right now.*

Oh, so Ruth was having her chat with me in her car and hadn't yet left the hotel property.

Did you bring me my energy? I asked him.

Yes, m'lady. As much as I could carry. I'll transfer it to you anon.

The energy surged through me. It wasn't much, but hopefully it would allow a simple spell or two. First, I needed to dissolve any strands of magic that bound me to the pen.

The white magic I practice creates spells that are woven like a tapestry or built from crystalline structures resembling snowflakes.

Black magic, however, is built more like flesh, with cells and fat and tendons. It's not pretty, and it decays over time.

I used the borrowed energy to activate magic that allowed me to visualize and alter the structure of the magic Ruth had used.

And then, dismantle it.

"What are you doing?" she asked, alarmed. "I sense magic. You shouldn't be able to use any magic."

With my limited senses, I felt a blast of whatever spell she was using to stop me. I worked quickly to deteriorate the fleshy structure of her spell.

Another blast rocked me. I couldn't feel physical pain, but the agony I felt could be described as psychic pain. And it was bad. I dropped my attempt to dismantle her spell and did my best to cast a protection spell. It wasn't very powerful, but all it had to protect was a woman living in a ballpoint pen.

Don Mateo! Please fetch me more energy. I need it badly.

I shall make as many trips as needed, m'lady. Like a fire brigade running with buckets of water.

"We can't even have an honest conversation, you and I,

without your being sneaky," Ruth said. "You ask me to give you more time to commit to joining my coven. But I know you'll betray me!"

I just want to return to my body. How would you like to be stuck inside a ballpoint pen?

The protection spell was holding up, and my psychic pain receded. Now, I returned to breaking her spell that imprisoned me. Don Mateo continually returned to me, pretty quickly, I might add, even for a ghost. The tiny bucket after bucket of energy gradually strengthened me.

"What are you doing?" Ruth shrieked. "It's time to destroy you once and for all. You'll be gone, and your body will be nothing more than a vegetable."

A new force hit me, much stronger than before. My protection spell was going to fail.

I quickly pulled apart the fleshy fibers and tendrils that supported Ruth's spell. The blasts of painful magic hitting me weakened.

"Come on!" Ruth said through clenched teeth. "You should be dead by now."

Her spell began falling apart. I felt less claustrophobic. The magic binding me inside the pen loosened.

"You witchy little—"

Out of spite, Ruth broke the ballpoint pen in half.

And suddenly, power rushed into me like wind into a sail. It was my innate, natural energy returning to me. The bond that tethered my consciousness to my body was intact again.

The ink from the pen splattered Ruth's face.

And I burst the bubble of my protection spell. A hurricane-force gust hit me, disorienting me, sending me flying

Until my eyes flitted open. My own eyes. I was in my body again, lying awkwardly in the passenger seat of Matt's truck

I groaned, and Matt jumped, turning to look at me.

"Holy moly, you're back!"

"Yeah, but Ruth is in her car in the same parking lot. Let's get out of here *now*!"

"Don Mateo appeared to me," Matt said as he sped away. "He said to stay close to the hotel. I thought I should get you to the ER, but I'm glad I did what he said."

"So am I. He harvested energy from my body and brought it to me."

"Um, where were you?"

"It's complicated. I'll explain later."

I told him about the worship meeting and how Ruth was planning to harass the business owners just like Dunott had.

"Maybe someone will take her out next," Matt said.

"And it appears that the Knights Simplar didn't kill Dunott. But the loup-garou doesn't know that. We should act like Arseton is our prime suspect to lure the loup-garou to him."

"Don't tell me you still want to capture this monster."

"I do," I said, though not convincingly enough.

"I think the Friends of Cryptids Society is going to get you killed. You've already done enough for them. Please tell them no."

"They promised to back me up."

"They can't arrive fast enough to save you if a loup-garou is about to rip your throat out."

"They're a non-profit. They do the best they can."

"That's not good enough."

"Then my magic will have to make up the difference."

CHAPTER 22
SHIFTING REALITIES

E very night before going to sleep, I thought about the monster. Yeah, I know, it was a recipe for nightmares, and I had more than a few. What I was trying to do was sense his psychic energy like I'd done before. It was my desperate attempt to locate him without using someone as bait and getting them killed.

I would lie in bed with the lights out, clear my head, focus on the energy frequency where I had sensed him before, and activate a bit of magic to heighten my sensitivity. Then, I would wait.

And wait.

And, eventually, fall asleep to encounter dreams of a half-man, half-wolf beast staring at me with glowing eyes that showed human intelligence, while below them was a wolf's muzzle with a drooling mouth and impossibly long canine teeth.

Except, tonight was different. Tonight, my entire body tingled as I connected with his psychic energy.

He was shifting to wolf form while being tormented by emotional distress. That's why his energy was so inflamed tonight.

Fragmentary images flew across my mind. I sensed he was in Jellyfish Beach, not too far from my house, and when I recognized one of the brief images, I realized where he was.

Georgette's new condo on the beach. I don't know why, but I just knew he was there to attack his sister-in-law.

I jumped out of bed, cats scattering to their hideaways, and called Matt while I threw on clothes.

"Meet me at Georgette's condo immediately," I told him. "Dunott's brother is shifting and about to attack her."

"You can't drive your car. You're missing a door."

"There's no time to pick me up. Meet me there."

I don't even know what his response was because I stuck the phone in my jeans and raced to my car.

I'm always saying derogatory things about the Jellyfish Beach Police Department. Tonight, I was pleased that they were understaffed and incompetent. Because I drove at double the speed limit through town, across the drawbridge to the beach, and down A1A, until I reached the condo building. And it would have been hard to miss me in my open-air seat. At least I was wearing my safety belt.

When I got off the elevator on Georgette's floor, I hurried to her door and cast a quick unlocking spell. Loud growling came from inside, followed by an eerie howl that made me tingle again because of how mournful it sounded.

Had he already killed her?

When the deadbolt clicked open, I realized I had no plan other than to use my immobility spell against the loup-garou. Matt and his silver bullets weren't here yet. But I couldn't wait.

I opened the door and saw no one. But I sensed two living creatures somewhere in here. Emphasis on two. Georgette was still alive.

Low, menacing growls came from the hallway to the bedrooms, and I moved in that direction, gathering my energies for the spells. My fear formed an icy spike in my stomach.

Reaching the entrance to the hall, I stayed out of view and peered around the corner.

At the far end of the hallway, the loup-garou in full wolf form crouched outside a closed bedroom door. He was whining, like a dog begging to be let inside. It wasn't what I had expected to see.

I assumed Georgette was inside the bedroom and had no doubt that Dunott's brother could smash through the door in seconds. If he wanted to. Even monsters had family ties, I realized. The monster was reluctant to kill his sister-in-law.

But why was he threatening her at all?

I could worry about that later. I had spells to cast.

First, I built a protection spell around me. I wasn't going to leave anything to chance. My sleep spell would have been fast and easy, but I'd learned at Furman's store that it didn't work on the loup-garou. Instead, I concentrated on the immobility spell. This time, I would cast it *before* he attacked me.

Gripping the Red Dragon talisman, feeling the warmth of its power infusing me, I combined its energy with those of the elements and from deep within me. I silently recited the incantation. The spell formed like a ball of invisible fire.

I stepped beyond the shelter of the wall and flung the spell down the hall at the monster.

He had sensed me and was turning to face me when the spell hit him. His body spasmed as if he were having a seizure. He collapsed onto the floor, whimpering.

I pulled out my phone and called Angela. Despite the hour, she answered instantly, as if expecting the call.

"I neutralized the loup-garou," I said breathlessly, giving her the address. "Please hurry."

The loup-garou was still. Wary of approaching him, I studied him from my end of the hallway. The wolf was twice as large as any wolf I'd seen in a zoo. Werewolves, which run slightly larger than wild wolves, were puny compared to this creature.

His coat was shiny black, streaked with gray, and his paws were the size of catcher's mitts, even without the long nails. He breathed unevenly, curled up with his head tucked beneath the nub of his tail. I'd never seen a wolf shifter with a full tail.

The bedroom door handle clicked as it was unlocked, and the door opened slightly. Georgette peered out, looking at the immobile loup-garou with surprise.

"You'd better stay locked in there," I said. "I'm a witch, and my magic neutralized him, but I don't know how long it will last. He's a powerful creature."

She shut the door, locking it again.

And my doubts about my spell came to fruition.

The loup-garou raised his head and stared at me with his yellow-rimmed eyes. His nostrils flared as he took in my scent.

Oh, crap.

He struggled to move his limbs, which meant the spell

hadn't completely failed, but it was clearly wearing off. He growled as he tried to get to his feet. I backed away until I was out of his line of sight, then sprinted toward the condo's front door.

My hand was just touching the doorknob when my protection bubble was struck by an immense force. I went flying into an entry table by the door, sending a lamp crashing onto the floor. I rolled over to find the loup-garou lunging at me.

The bubble saved me from the snapping, slavering jaws, but they seemed to get closer to me with each thrust. I screamed. I'm not the screaming type, but to have this monster only a couple of feet away, pinning me in my bubble to the floor as I felt the bubble weaken, was horrifying.

It was like being in a shark cage while a Great White battered it repeatedly and the steel bars were giving way.

There were no potent offensive spells in my armory. I was good at protecting and healing with magic, not attacking and harming. Maybe I should have given in to my mother and learned black magic.

The only thing I could do was pump more energy into my protection spell and try to get out of the condo with the hope the monster wouldn't kill me in the public areas. Meanwhile, I was stuck on my back like a turtle.

A high-pitched growling cry came from the direction of the bedrooms. Great. Is there another monster here trying to kill me?

Or had Georgette shifted? That cry didn't sound like it came from a werewolf, though.

Something tan flashed through the corner of my eye, and

suddenly the loup-garou was off me and thrashing about in a battle with a large animal.

A Florida panther.

The loup-garou was larger, but the panther was inflicting serious damage with its slashing claws, trying to disembowel the wolf. The two predators circled each other, then engaged with jaws and claws, and ended up wrestling on the floor. This cycle repeated, and each animal had wounds that weren't supernaturally healing as quickly as I would've thought.

But with the loup-garou distracted, I got back on my feet and tried again to get out the front door. I grabbed the doorknob.

As I did, the door swung inward, smashing into my bubble, and knocking me to the floor again.

It was Matt, his eyes wide open in shock.

"I've got the worst timing," he said.

"No, you don't! Let's get out of here." I pushed past him and out the door.

"Oh, no!" Matt shouted. He pulled out his gun with a trembling hand and almost dropped it.

The loup-garou was leaping toward him. The panther tried to tackle the wolf.

Matt fired a shot, the sharp retort echoing inside my protection bubble.

The panther gave a growling scream and fell on its side. The loup-garou changed course mid-leap and flew over Matt instead of into him. The massive creature landed beside me in the exterior hallway, but kept going, bounding down the corridor past the other units.

At the end of the corridor was a window. The monster smashed through it and disappeared.

"We're four floors above the ground," I said, though no one was listening.

Matt stared at the panther, and I came closer so I could see her. She still lay on her side on the living room floor with a bullet wound on her flank. Before our eyes, the wound slowly healed.

The panther returned to her feet, sniffed the air, then trotted back toward the bedrooms. She turned to make brief eye contact with me before going into the hallway.

I heard the bedroom door close, and the lock click.

"I want to see if the loup-garou survived the fall," I said, heading down the exterior corridor.

I stuck my head through the broken window, curtains billowing beside me, and looked down. The ground below was a manicured lawn and shrubs with no sign of a wolf.

"He made it," I said.

I walked back to the condo, and the elevator dinged. When its doors opened, Angela walked out, carrying her mage's staff. I guessed that was her heavy artillery. Two male workers in white jumpsuits followed, one carrying a rolled-up tarp and the other pushing a handcart.

"Everyone's running a little late tonight," I said.

"What happened?" Angela asked. "Did the creature escape?"

"Yep. I think he was here to attack Dunott's widow. But then he came after me. When Matt showed up with the silver bullets, he escaped."

Angela glared at Matt. "The loup-garou was supposed to be captured alive."

"It overcame my immobility spell," I explained. "I was helpless to do anything when the monster came closer and closer to breaching my protection spell."

"Was the creature shot?"

"Not the loup-garou. The were-panther was shot. The silver bullet was enough to scare the loup-garou away, though."

"Were-panther?"

"Yeah. Mrs. Dunott, the widow. She's in the bedroom. She attacked the loup-garou and probably saved my life. I had sensed that she was a shifter, but assumed she was a werewolf or loup-garou."

"I guess silver doesn't harm other sorts of shifters," Matt said.

"That would be correct," said Angela.

"She could have been the woman who bought the silver bullets from Brian Bartman," I suggested. "We need to have a chat with her."

I walked to the master bedroom with Angela and Matt behind me.

"Mrs. Dunott, we need to ask you some questions," I shouted, knocking on the door. "Mrs. Dunott? Please."

I tried the handle, already knowing it was locked. Instead of casting a spell to unlock it, I just kicked the door in. It was one of those nights.

The master suite was empty, curtains blowing beside the open window.

Apparently, were-panthers could survive four-story jumps, too.

"Is she a new suspect for Dunott's murder?" Matt asked.

"Maybe. We've been wrong about every other suspect, so we shouldn't jump to conclusions. I'd really like some more evidence."

"The loup-garou—Dunott's brother—was here to attack her," Matt said. "He wasn't waiting for us to suspect her."

"Too bad we can't talk to him."

"Oh, yes you can," Angela said. "You still need to capture him. Then, you can ask all the questions you want."

"I can't capture him with the spells I have."

"I'll teach you another one. A real doozy of a spell."

CHAPTER 23
TO CATCH A MONSTER

It was highly unlikely that the loup-garou would go to Georgette's condo again, and we didn't know where she was. So, our best strategy for trapping him was to hope he went after a different suspect.

Ever since we first suspected the Knights Simplar to have killed Dunott, I'd been going through the same play-acting routine I had previously used to lure the monster to Furman's store. Now, though, it was centered on Arseton.

I felt badly putting Furman's life in danger, now that I knew he was innocent. In this case, Arseton was also innocent—if you believed his words—but I didn't feel as guilty about putting him in peril. After all, the lunatic had tried to kill several who were dear to me.

I continued this effort after the battle at the condo. Matt and I had talked a lot about Arseton, pretending we believed he was the actual murderer, debating if he was in cahoots with Georgette. And I thought about him constantly, conjuring up mental images of him at the repair store. I'd rather the loup-garou show up there than Arseton's apartment, where the attack could come at any time during the night. At the store, the monster would have a limited window of opportunity.

The window was so narrow, in fact, that I didn't rely on my psychic connection to alert me to the monster's movements. Instead, I staked out the store every night around closing time. The monster was known to only attack at night, and the final hours leading up to closing time were when fewer witnesses would be around.

I did so even though Angela hadn't yet taught me the new spell she had promised would be more effective against the monster. However, we'd already sown the seeds of Arseton being guilty, and the loup-garou may have already read our minds. He might attack Arseton any night now, so I had to keep an eye on the store.

Matt, of course, wouldn't allow me to do it alone, so each night, we sat together in my newly rented car; me getting my magic warmed up to be ready in an instant, and him clutching his pistol with the two remaining silver bullets.

Needless to say, no one's thoughts turned to romance. With our focus on a dork who gave himself the title of Lord and a terrifying monster, making out in the front seat was just not going to happen.

Speaking of dorks, I still had the nasty tissue that had cleaned up Arseton's spittle. I made the quick decision to cast my altered penetration spell when a man with black clothing entered You Break It, We'll Try to Fix It. Closing time was in only a few minutes, and Arseton's assistant had just left for the night.

The man who entered the store was Dunott's twin brother, paying a visit to Arseton in human form instead of assaulting him in wolf form. Maybe, after all the false suspects he had killed, he wanted to ask questions before he tore Arseton to pieces.

I texted Angela that I was about to encounter the monster again.

Clutching my power charm, I cast the spell. The audio and visuals, coming from a perspective just above Arseton's head, turned on in mid-conversation.

"No, you had learned werewolves really do exist *before* I saw you in Furman's shop," Dunott's brother said. "You were planning to kill my brother Pierre because he was a werewolf."

Claude reached out and grabbed Arseton's shirt before his brave lordship could run away.

He was Dunott's identical twin, but he looked more slovenly than I'd ever seen the commissioner. The brother's black hair was dirty, and he had gone several days without shaving. There were dark circles under his eyes. Murdering innocent people must have been stressful. Poor guy.

"No. I didn't know your brother was a werewolf," Arseton said nervously. "Was he killed with a silver bullet?"

"Yes. Quite a coincidence that you have silver bullets, isn't it? They're not exactly common. Why do you have them?"

"For protection. My order battles monsters. But you've got to believe me. I didn't kill him. I had no intention of killing him."

"You were going to kill Furman."

"No, I swear!"

Claude's face displayed signs he was about to shift. His skin grew flushed, his jaw muscles pulsated, and his eyelids twitched.

Arseton must not have recognized the signs, or he didn't have his gun with the silver bullets handy. He just stood there, although Claude had released his hold on Arseton's shirt as he prepared for shifting.

I needed to go in before it was too late.

Releasing the spell, I told Matt what I was going to do and exited the car before he could convince me not to. I ran across the parking lot to the store, but didn't go in yet, so I could prepare my calming spell.

As Angela had advised me, I held the Red Dragon talisman that I now always carried in my pocket, along with my power charm. The small bronze cylinder grew warm while my energies surged.

Claude noticed me just outside of the door. Fur was already sprouting from his face and hands. He looked at me curiously while Arseton stood behind the counter, his mouth open in amazement at the shifting process.

I recited the calming spell's incantation and included the words *non mutare manent absolutem.* I sent forth the magic.

Dunott's brother convulsed and fell to the floor in great pain. I opened the door and stepped inside.

"What did you do to me?" he cried as his face spasmed.

But he didn't transform into a wolf. He remained in the early stage of shifting, the new fur still on his skin but not growing anymore.

I cast my immobility spell, and the man went still, but his eyes still showed his pain. Matt arrived and stood guard outside the door.

"I'll do something about your pain shortly," I told him. "But first, you must answer some questions."

Now, I cast my truth-telling spell and sprinkled the powder on him. Rarely had I cast multiple spells at once, and I admit I was feeling weakened from all the energy I had expended.

"Tell me," I said, "are you the one who killed Leticia, Damian, and Boris?"

"Yes."

"Why?"

"For revenge."

"Did you choose them because you knew they were suspects?"

"Yes," he said through gritted teeth. "I read your mind."

I felt horrible pangs of guilt as my suspicions that he had done this were confirmed.

"But why did you keep killing people I suspected when it turned out I was wrong?"

"Because I didn't think you'd be so wrong so often."

I hung my head in shame.

"And," he continued, "even if they weren't murderers, it was clear that they had thought about doing it. I killed them to punish them for their disloyalty to me."

"What?" I couldn't make sense of what he was saying. "What do you mean disloyalty to you?"

He tried to smile, but winced in pain.

"I'm Pierre Dunott," he said.

I was dumbfounded. "You're *Pierre*?"

"My brother, Claude, was killed because he's my identical twin."

"They thought they were murdering you, but killed him by mistake?"

He winced with pain and nodded.

"Was he a loup-garou, too?" I asked.

"Yes."

"Why was he in your bedroom?"

"He had come to town to visit us. The killers must have dragged him into our bedroom after shooting him."

"This is crazy," I said. "They killed your brother by mistake, and you said nothing about it to the police or anyone else?"

"No. Pretending I'm dead allows me incredible freedom. Soon, I'll kill the murderer. And I'm weeding out all the troublemakers in town, so the werewolves will be completely loyal to me when I reappear and take control of the pack again. And kooks like this phone-repair guy won't be a danger to my pack."

"Where have you been staying?"

"In hotels."

"Does your wife know about this?"

"Yes. And she's followed my orders to keep it secret."

"Why did you attack her the other night?"

"I went to her condo not to attack her, but to . . . straighten out some things."

"Tell me," I commanded. "What did you want from her?"

"Honesty. I wanted honesty from her. She told me she didn't know who murdered Claude, but I've suspected more and more that she does. Why would she not tell me?"

"Have you ever suspected her of being unfaithful to you?"

"She would never do that," he argued. "Never."

Watching him writhing in pain was really getting to me,

bringing out my nursing instincts, but I tried to remain focused.

"Would you by any chance consider speaking with the Friends of Cryptids Society of the Americas?" I asked, rather foolishly. "They would love to examine a loup-garou. It's for the good of your species and all supernatural creatures."

"No! Take this spell, or whatever you did, off me!"

I hadn't thought he'd say yes.

He moaned, and empathy for his suffering clenched my heart.

"I'll help you take a little nap, so you won't feel the pain."

Figuring the sleep spell would work on him because he hadn't fully shifted, I released the truth spell while keeping the other spells going so he wouldn't be a threat. Next, I began casting the sleep spell, though juggling three spells was exhausting me.

He moaned piteously. Without thinking, I reached out to stroke his forehead to comfort him.

Big mistake. I hadn't realized my immobility spell was weakening.

Dunott tilted his head and bit my hand.

Yes, he used human, not infectious wolf, teeth. They didn't break my skin. But the pain jolted me. I cried out and everything went wrong at once. My equilibrium was knocked astray, my concentration was gone, my energies became jumbled, and my spells fell apart like shattered glass.

Dunott pushed me backward, and before anyone else could react, he jumped up and ran around the counter into the back of the store. The rear door's banging meant that he was gone.

"Why didn't you stop him?" I asked Arseton.

He babbled an attempt at an answer. The fact was, he had been terrified.

I ran past him, through the workshop and an office, then out the back door. The only lighting back there was small lamps beside each store's back door. A couple of dumpsters sat behind the strip center, but no cars were parked there. I looked to my right and left but saw no one.

To the right was a fence and an apartment complex on the other side. To the left was a small parcel of woods.

Since Dunott had come into the store in human form, I assumed he had driven here. I needed to hurry to the front of the strip center to see if I could spot him running to his car.

A branch snapped in the woods. The tingling that signaled supernatural activity spread through me. And there, deep in the shadows of the woods, two yellow eyes glowed.

Dunott had completed his transformation into wolf or half-wolf. No way was I going to attempt to capture him with my magic having failed me and my energies in disarray.

Until we meet again, loup-garou, I thought.

I returned to the store to find Matt standing by the front door, his pistol useless in his hand.

"What happened to your magic?" he asked.

"Don't you dare ask."

"Daughter of Saint Ruthless," Arseton said, "you need to join her coven and learn stronger magic."

His fearful expression had been replaced by a smirk.

"Let's go, Matt," I said.

As soon as we left the store, I gave Arseton a little magical present. My stink-bomb spell. I glanced back as we reached my car to see him through the window, scurrying about with a rag pressed to his nose and mouth.

I called Angela and told her that the night had been a bust.

"I need you to teach me that new spell as soon as possible," I said. "Please?"

"Come by my house Saturday morning. Bring the Red Dragon."

My desire was no longer just to capture the loup-garou. Now that I knew Dunott was alive, and he knew how weak my magic was on him, my greatest desire was to stay alive.

CHAPTER 24
MAGIC LESSONS

Of course, they were waiting for me when I got home. Mrs. Lupis and Mr. Lopez.

"Can I offer you any tea or coffee or antifreeze?" I asked as I pushed past them to unlock the front door.

"Details are all we ask for," Mr. Lopez replied. "Angela told us you failed tonight."

I shouldn't have let it get to me, but it did.

"I did not fail. My magic enabled us to turn this case around. The only thing I didn't do was capture the loup-garou, which, frankly, was an absurd request by you guys. Are you freaking crazy? I, a home-health nurse, botanica owner, and middling witch, am supposed to capture one of the world's most fearsome monsters? What were you thinking?"

"We have the utmost confidence in you," Mrs. Lupis said.

"Unreasonable confidence. I mean, Angela has twice as much power as I. Maybe more. Why do I have to do this alone?"

"You have your reporter friend."

"I'm talking about magic! Why do I have to do the dirty, dangerous work, and then Angela simply shows up for the extraction? It makes no sense."

"You've heard the term 'cannon fodder'?" Mr. Lopez asked, trying to be cute but ticking me off even more.

"Exactly. That's all I am to you."

"Need we remind you that Angela is in her seventies?" Mrs. Lupis asked.

"And that she is handling several urgent assignments?" Mr. Lopez added.

"I know. But she has twice the magic I do. What's the point of sacrificing your 'cannon fodder' while innocent people are being killed?"

"Angela is powerful, yes," said Mrs. Lupis. "She is deadly while on the offensive. But at her age, she's not so great on the defensive. She's not as nimble and inventive as you."

"Don't try to flatter me."

"We can't afford to lose Angela," Mr. Lopez said.

"Ah, so now the truth comes out. I'm expendable, and she isn't."

"That's not what I meant."

"Why don't you give us a download of where you are with the case?" Mrs. Lupis said, trying to refocus the conversation.

I recounted our haphazard journey through suspects—and how they were, one by one, killed by the loup-garou that we had thought was Dunott's brother. When I told them it was the brother who was murdered, and not Dunott, Mrs. Lupis and Mr. Lopez were shocked.

"I did not see that coming," Mrs. Lupis said.

"We knew there was a twin," said her partner. "You have to expect a plot twist when twins are involved."

I added that Angela's magic-spell suggestion enabled me to halt the loup-garou's shifting process, albeit only temporarily. And that she would teach me a new, more powerful spell to use against the monster.

"I'm pleased that you're making progress," Mr. Lopez said. He sounded like a difficult-to-please parent.

"What's the next step in the murder investigation?" Mrs. Lupis asked.

Various tiny hints and clues had finally coalesced in my mind.

"We need to look into Dunott's wife. She knew her husband wasn't murdered, but she didn't tell us. I believe there's a lot more she's keeping secret."

"Sounds promising. Keep us informed of any developments."

"And do try to stay alive," Mr. Lopez added with a twinkle in his eye.

"How kind of you to say."

SATURDAY WAS a day off from the botanica, and Angela had asked me to come to her house early. Dawn was just breaking when I arrived, and the lake behind her house was fringed with mist. A great blue heron glided out of the fog while unseen limpkins cried mournfully from the lakeshore.

When Angela greeted me at her front door, I smelled cheesy eggs, bacon, fresh bread, and more.

"First, we'll have a big breakfast," she said. "Proteins, carbs, and fats to convert into energy. And lots of salt."

"Salt?"

"Yes, it's not good for you, but it helps amplify elemental magic and fight black magic. Why? I have never figured that out."

We devoured the hearty feast while she encouraged me to down several cups of tea and water.

"Caffeine and hydration are helpful, too," she explained.

"Do sports drinks help?"

"Yes. But not sugary ones. Someone should design a sports drink specifically for magic practitioners."

"That would be a perfect product to sell in the botanica," I said, my mind racing with merchandising ideas. If only I had the time to develop such a product.

After we ate and cleaned up, Angela led me into her backyard.

"I will spend the day teaching you the spell. But it really takes months to be proficient at it, and years to master it. We simply don't have the luxury of that much time."

"If I ran into the loup-garou, say tomorrow, would I be able to use the spell against him?"

"Yes. If you are completely focused and at the top of your game. Otherwise, it could fail."

That concerned me. It is rather difficult to focus when you're about to be eaten by a mega-werewolf.

"Have you used this spell against werewolves before?" I asked.

"No."

"No?"

"I've been developing it for some time, but it's not designed specifically to fight werewolves. It's designed for you."

"Oh. Thank you. But you don't even know if it works?"

"Oh, it works. I believe in it, and you must, too. Believing is a fundamental tenet of magic, dear."

"Yeah, I know. I just happen to be a witch without a lot of self-confidence."

"You need to get beyond that if you want to be truly powerful. Now, let us begin. To aid the spell—and to give you confidence—you will wear this amulet."

She reached up and draped a leather cord attached to a small leather pouch over my neck. It smelled funny.

"This contains silver flakes, dried wolf's bane, dead fleas, and a small amount of timber-wolf urine."

"Are you serious?"

"The urine sends the message, 'This is my territory. Go away.' The other ingredients are self-explanatory. The amulet has been empowered with protection and warding spells. You can wear it with the other amulet, the one that disrupts the monster's shifting."

"Thank you," I said, even though the amulet's odor was making my eyes water.

"Now comes the difficult part. Attack magic."

"Oh, I don't know. I've always been a pacifist. You know, healing magic and whatnot."

"I'm not talking about black magic," Angela said slowly, drilling me with her stare. "You've seen for yourself that your defensive magic does not work to neutralize the beast. You need to knock him out of action. Like the fireballs you've seen me shoot. Nothing evil about them. They come from elemental magic. We need to see which elements you have the most affinity for."

"I use all five in my magic."

"Of course. But you derive more strength from one or more."

"Earth, I would say."

"Let's confirm that. Relax and give me a moment."

We faced each other at a patio table beside her pool. She took my left hand in her right and placed her left hand atop my head. Her eyes closed, and I felt energy thrum through my head and hand. Several minutes later, she released me.

"Yes, you are closely aligned to the earth and air elements. Not so much fire or water, but you also have a strong connection with spirit. For me, I'm most aligned with fire, which is why I use fireballs. I'm going inside to consult my grimoires. Come join me. If we're lucky, I can come up with two spells for you."

I spent an hour watching her leaf through old leather-bound tomes in her upstairs loft. At one point, she giggled.

"Oh, this will be good," she said with a big smile.

Finally, she closed the last grimoire, causing a cloud of dust.

"At first, I thought of making you a magic wand," she said. "But I remembered you have the Red Dragon. That's more powerful than any wand."

"How should I use it?"

"As usual, to strengthen and concentrate your spells. The new spells you will learn draw upon the earth and air. A windstorm spell, and a seismic spell," she said proudly.

"Wow," I whispered as I imagined the potential.

"With practice, you'll be able to attack opponents with wind gusts and even tornadoes and hurricane-force winds. There's very little seismic activity in Florida, but with the second spell, you'll be able to harness the energy of the earth to create sinkholes and mini earthquakes. You'll be quite formidable. If, that is, you can cast the spells correctly."

Right, I thought, if I'm not too panicked by the monster who's seconds away from eating my face.

"Now," Angela said, "it's time for school."

Learning spells requires much more than memorizing incantations. But that's where it begins, which isn't easy if Latin or other ancient languages are involved. You have to get the pronunciations correct, based on how each word would have been spoken centuries ago.

Next, Angela gave me a literature class on how many of the lines of the incantations contained double-entendres and metaphors. The spell caster had to take these meanings into account; otherwise, she'd just be reciting empty words with no power.

The sounds of the words had acoustic effects, which were important, too. They conjured up images in my head and inspired emotions in my heart, which were even more important. All of this contributed to triggering the magic.

Most crucial of all was how the words channeled energy into the cosmos, turning the energy into magic. Angela spent several hours teaching me how to get the maximum energy from the earth and air elements.

In the past, I had gathered energy from all five elements all at once rather haphazardly. Today, Angela taught me how to gather my own energy and then use it to drill into only one element, harvesting it in all its depth and complexity.

I was lucky to be able to leverage my telekinesis. My previous training with Angela had strengthened it, so it was now useful for more than stopping my phone from falling to the ground. It had become critical for enhancing spells that involved moving things in the physical world.

The spells Angela taught me today required lots of moving. Creating a windstorm or shaking a tectonic plate involved greater force, and my telekinesis helped me direct the elemental powers to achieve this.

Angela showed me how to incorporate my telekinesis into the spells seamlessly and instinctually. Casting the spell would automatically activate my telekinesis, and I didn't have to distract myself by thinking about it. Importantly, she reminded me that my telekinesis could not stop a loup-garou on its own. That's where the elemental magic came in.

"It's time for practical exercises," Angela announced. "Let's go to the front yard and see if you can conjure up some seismic events."

"You want me to create an earthquake? Does your insurance cover that?"

"No, dear. All you need to do is move a little dirt."

Angela had a lanai by her front door, covered with a vine-draped trellis. A hedge shielded the lanai from the view of passersby. I knelt on the tiles in a small magic circle, which Angela allowed but encouraged me to learn to do without. I wouldn't have the luxury of drawing a magic circle if I were being chased by a loup-garou.

There was no pentagram representing the five elements

because I was drawing upon only one: earth. I gathered my innate energies, enabled by the magic in my DNA, then used them to home in on the power of the earth beneath me, the soil, the plants growing in it, the strata of rock beneath it all descending miles below me.

Then, I used the Red Dragon talisman, burning hot in my hand, to concentrate the energies and direct them outward.

The paver bricks at the end of Angela's driveway buckled upward before settling down.

"Good!" Angela said. "Keep going."

Without breaking my concentration, I directed more power toward the end of her driveway. A light post beside the driveway trembled. I gave it some more juice. The light post shook back and forth, faster, and faster, and fell over, pulling its concrete base and wiring from the dirt.

Before I could apologize, Angela told me to keep going.

I did. And soon, the large oak tree that shaded her lawn quivered and her mailbox vibrated. A rumbling sound reached me, and I felt the vibrations in my feet and knees.

"Okay, Missy. I think that's good—"

With a deafening crunch, the asphalt in the street broke apart just as a UPP delivery van drove over it. Suddenly, the van disappeared.

In its place was a chasm in the middle of the street. I had caused one of Florida's notorious sinkholes.

"Oops," I said. "Should we call nine-one-one?"

The UPP driver crawled out of the hole and scratched his head while he looked down at his van in the hole.

"He's fine," Angela replied. "Let's try some wind exercises."

We passed through the house and out to the swimming pool area.

"Let's see you whip up some wind on the surface of the pool," Angela said. "Someday, when you've mastered this spell, you'll be able to create full-fledged waterspouts, tornadoes, and more. But for now, let's keep it simple."

I went through the spell-casting process again, this time focusing on the air element. As the power surged through me, it felt different from what had come from the earth. It felt, well, airy.

With the Red Dragon in hand, I directed it to the water in the pool.

Ripples spread across the surface as a gentle breeze blew.

I pumped out more energy. The breeze turned into a sharp gust, and the far end of the pool grew choppy. Angela's alligator pool float took flight and landed in her neighbor's yard.

"Good," she said.

The power was pouring out of me like a jet engine. I couldn't turn it down and feared I was losing control. Pulling my focus away from the pool, I aimed across the lawn, toward the lake.

Distant palm trees twitched, and white caps appeared on the lake.

"You can stop now," Angela said.

No, I couldn't. I tried, though.

The sight of a jet skier soaring by twenty feet in the air shocked me enough to regain control. The power ebbed, and I released the spell.

"Oh my," I said. "What happened to the jet skier?"

"See that house across the way? He landed in their swim-ming pool. He'll be fine. I hate jet skis. They're so noisy."

She smiled and patted me on my arm.

"Congratulations on learning two spells with a lot of poten-tial," she said.

"Thank you for teaching me. But how, exactly, will these spells defeat a loup-garou?"

"I don't know. You'll find out when you need to."

Something told me I would need to very soon.

CHAPTER 25
NO-TELL MOTEL

I didn't know if Dunott had given up on Matt and me solving his brother's murder. He might still be following me, reading my mind. But it seemed like that would be a waste of time.

Because we were investigating a suspect Dunott had already become suspicious of: his wife.

Not surprisingly, she appeared to have moved out of her condo. She never answered when we rang her bell, and we ran into a resident who said she hadn't been seen in several days.

Or, perhaps, her husband had taken her away. We had no way of knowing, so we spent a lot of time parked outside of the coffee shop where Dunott's assistant, Greg Ackney, held court.

Finally, it paid off. One morning, Georgette parked her luxury car nearby and went inside.

I didn't have items from anyone that would enable me to use my surveillance spell to spy on her. I didn't want to use my penetration spell and stand outside the historic building with my hands against the wall in this highly visible location. So, I used regular human spy craft—I peered through binoculars at the front windows of the cafe. I saw Georgette talking with Ackney and Judy, the owner.

"What are they doing?" Matt asked.

"Talking. Obviously, I can't hear them."

"You need to learn more magic spells."

"You need to learn more reporting skills."

"That's not fair!" he said, pouting.

"It's not fair to expect my magic to solve everything. I'm just a witch. I'm not the Wizard of Oz."

"At least we can follow her and, hopefully, find out where she's staying."

Which was what we did after she left the coffee shop. Surprisingly, her next stop was The Cat's Meow, Furman's boutique. Furman's shed hairs, which I had used in my spell to spy on him previously, had been drained of his psychic energy, so they were useless. All we could do was speculate about why she was here. Who knows, maybe were-panthers like catnip.

She soon left, with a shopping bag in hand. I'm sure it was catnip. Next, she went to a sandwich shop and exited with a large bag.

"Looks like a lot of food in there," Matt said. "She must be meeting a person or persons."

We expected her to head to the beach or a park, but she continued north, away from town. Eventually, she pulled into a one-story mom-and-pop motel, a holdover from the old days of Florida tourism. The place wasn't a dump like where the hitman had been staying, but it was nowhere near the level of luxury I'd expect of Georgette.

We parked along the curb right before we got to the motel's parking lot, where we had an unobstructed view of the place.

She approached the door of a unit in the middle of the row, and someone unseen opened it for her from the inside. She slipped in with the sandwiches, and the door closed.

"This certainly looks suspicious," I said.

"It appears that Pierre was not the only one being unfaithful."

"This means she had motive to kill her husband because he was cheating on her, or because she wanted to marry her paramour."

"Or both," Matt said.

"Do you really think she could have killed Dunott's brother by mistake? That she couldn't tell the twins apart? No," I said after thinking it through, "she knew her brother-in-law was visiting. That means the paramour probably did it."

"That makes more sense. How do we find out who the paramour is?"

"In this case, I can use my penetration spell. I'll go behind the hotel where no one can see me. It might take a while for me to see who it is, if they've got the lights off in there, so be patient."

I got out and walked past the motel. It was a simple rectangular building facing south, perpendicular to the street. There were only eight units with a small office at the far end. There was no swimming pool at an establishment like this.

The rear of the motel was close to the property line, with a fence separating it from an auto-body shop next door. Between the fence and the motel was a thin strip of weeds and litter. Stacks of aluminum hurricane shutters leaned against the motel. The only windows were the small, frosted-glass panes of bathrooms. Above them were exhaust-fan vents.

No one driving by would notice me, so I went to the fourth window, placed my palms against the wall, and cast the spell.

When the spell penetrated the concrete block wall and the images appeared in my mind, I was disappointed. All I could see was the bathroom and part of a dressing alcove. Well, I would just have to wait until the lovebirds used the bathroom.

It didn't take as long as I had feared. When the paramour wearing only boxer shorts walked into the bathroom, I was shocked when I recognized him.

It was Stuart McDougall.

Georgette Dunott was involved with her husband's political opponent?

When he finished his business, he got into the shower. Let's just say I was not impressed with his body. It showed evidence of gym attendance, but also too much restaurant attendance.

More importantly, I identified him as a normal human with no supernatural in him. A human who had somehow managed to attract a were-panther.

I released the spell and went back to the car to tell Matt what I'd learned.

"That's crazy," Matt said. "I wonder if she hooked up with him after the murder, but before she found out that it was her brother-in-law, not her husband, who was killed."

"You're trying awfully hard to excuse her. When I saw it was McDougall, I remembered a minor fact: Ackney had said McDougall visited Dunott's home office on more than one occasion."

"So?"

"He knows the home and its layout. And I bet he visited there many times when Dunott wasn't home."

"We would need evidence of that. You're saying McDougall intended to murder Dunott so he and Georgette could be together?"

"Obviously," I said. "And probably for Dunott's life insurance, too. It would be plenty for the two of them to live off. And they could use the home-insurance payoff for the fire to buy a love nest. But he accidentally killed Dunott's brother instead. He'd probably never met him and couldn't tell the twins apart."

"You're going to have to use your truth-telling spell for him to admit that. And I don't think the spell would work on a lawyer."

"He won't even meet with us, so finding an opportunity to use the spell might be a little difficult. We'll go talk to Ackney again. But first, I want to follow Georgette after she leaves the motel. I have a hard time believing she's living here, and I want to find out where she's staying."

About an hour later, she left the motel and drove away, and we followed from a safe distance behind her. Surprisingly, she ended up in her old neighborhood, driving past her blackened home where renovations had already begun.

She pulled into the driveway of the same neighbor's home where she had stayed after the fire. She went inside carrying shopping bags and didn't come out. We waited until we grew bored.

"Yeah, she's probably staying here again, temporarily," Matt said.

"Which explains why she had to meet McDougall in a

motel. He can't come here, and she can't visit wherever he lives because of his wife."

We drove back to the coffee shop. I can't say I was surprised that Ackney was still there hours later. I had gotten the impression when we first met him that with his boss deceased, Ackney's job was to pretend to be well-connected by being in public as much as possible. And hopefully having others buy his coffee.

Paying for his cappuccino was exactly what we did. And while the large man sipped and preened with self-importance, I cast the truth-telling spell upon him.

His eyes gleamed with caffeine and the magically induced desire to unburden himself.

"Greg, is Pierre Dunott still alive?" I asked, hoping to confirm the shifting loup-garou had told the truth under my truth spell the other night.

"Why would you ask something like that after a horrible tragedy?"

"Well?"

"Yes. He's alive because his twin brother was accidentally killed instead of him."

"Dunott's pretending to be dead?"

"Yeah. For the life insurance and to get revenge on everyone who wanted to kill him."

"Have you spoken to him recently?"

"Sure. I'm his eyes and ears."

"Have your eyes and ears learned who killed his brother?"

"I just hang out here all day and listen to gossip."

"Does the gossip include who killed him?"

"Everyone assumes a local business owner did it. That's what Mr. Dunott thinks."

"What about Stuart McDougall? Do you think he did it?"

Ackney looked confused. "No. Why would he? Just because Mr. Dunott beat him in the election? There wasn't any bad blood between them."

"Did you know McDougall is having an affair with Georgette Dunott?" I asked, sprinkling a bit more powder beneath the table.

His eyes widened in surprise. "No. Are you serious?"

"Yes. I take it, then, that Mr. Dunott did not know about the affair."

"I don't think he would've kept it a secret from me. And he would have made McDougall's life miserable."

"Do you know where Mr. Dunott is living now?"

"No. He won't tell me, for my protection and his. We meet up at different places."

"Does Mr. Dunott have a large life insurance policy?"

"Yes. More than one. His wife has put in a claim and is waiting to collect. I asked her today about how she is getting by financially."

Some things have been bothering me about Dunott and his story. Had he been completely honest with me when I used the truth spell on him? The spell has been dependable over the years, especially with not-so-bright people like Ackney.

But if Dunott's supernatural powers were strong enough to defeat my other spells, could that mean my truth spell wasn't completely effective, as well?

"Let me ask you, Greg," I said. "Were there any criminal cases against Mr. Dunott? I understand that the local business owners were suing him and trying to instigate a federal civil-rights case."

His eyes widened with the desire to speak, while part of him fought the urge. The urge won.

"Yeah, the Feds were putting together a racketeering case against him. For, um, taking contributions from the local merchants."

"Contributions, you call them?"

"Uh, yeah. And the Feds were about to indict him."

"I see."

"Do you know where McDougall and his wife live?"

"I heard they recently bought a condo on the beach. Nice place, I bet."

He gave me the address. It was the same condo tower where Georgette had been living since the fire. How convenient and discreet for her to live in the same building as her lover.

Until Dunott—and we—showed up and ruined it. Now the two lovers had to meet in sordid motels to keep their relationship secret.

"How often do you see Mr. Dunott these days?" I asked.

"Just about every night. We catch up on stuff."

"Does he still pay you?"

"Um, not exactly. But he will when his life insurance pays out."

"Thank you for your help, Greg. I'll buy you another coffee. And I command you to say nothing about this conversation."

"I won't."

To make sure, I cast a forgetfulness spell, a close cousin to my truth spell.

I got up to get the coffee, and Matt left. When I returned with the cup, Ackney looked at me with surprise.

"Oh, hi! Nice to see you again," he said. "You bought that for me? You didn't have to do that, but you're so kind."

"You looked like you would appreciate it," I said before walking out.

"I'm worried about McDougall," I said to Matt when I got into the car.

"Why? If he killed Dunott's brother, he deserves to go to prison."

"He doesn't deserve to be torn to pieces by a loup-garou. Dunott already suspects his wife's been unfaithful, which is why he was at her condo when we showed up. It's only a matter of time until he finds out that she and McDougall are having an affair. We need to protect McDougall."

"If Dunott takes him out, we don't have to worry about whether our incompetent police and district attorney will successfully prosecute him for murdering the man he thought was Dunott."

"Dunott doesn't have the right to give him the death penalty. And I, for one, don't want to contribute to anyone else getting murdered."

"Ah, yes. I agree. So, how exactly do we stop Dunott?" Matt asked.

"He got into the condo building the other night because he was in human form and was a guest of his wife. But she's not there anymore, and McDougall won't allow security to let him in. He'll have to ambush McDougall somewhere."

"Can you use that spell Angela gave you to locate Dunott?"

"It works best when he's trying to connect with me telepathically. He was doing that to find out who we suspected was the murderer—those who were disloyal to him. If he finds out about his wife and McDougall, he'll be too occupied with that to bother with me."

"It won't work?"

"I had tried to become familiar with Dunott's psychic energy from his telepathic connections with me, so I might be able to get a general idea of his location even when we aren't connected. We'll see. Let me stop home to feed Tony and the cats, and I'll work on it."

After I took care of my witch's familiar and my fur babies, I made Matt wait in the living room while I stayed in the kitchen. The original amulet that alerted me to Dunott's telepathy was the key, so I removed my vampire-repellant amulet I almost always wear, and the newer one she gave me to protect me from Dunott, so they wouldn't interfere. Besides, wearing too many amulets made me look like a crazy witch lady.

Next, I reverted to my comfort zone and knelt inside a magic circle on the floor. Relying on all five elements would be helpful and reassuring. I clutched the amulet, cleared my mind, and used all my senses and intuition to search for Dunott's psychic energy.

I sensed him out there, somewhere. But I couldn't tell where. I improvised a variation of my locator spell, hoping it would lock into Dunott's energy, faint as it was.

I wasn't expecting a precise image of his location, like the locator spell would give me, but I sensed he was at or near the beach. Forcing more energy into the spell, I was hit by the scent of saltwater and wet sand. And the smell of motor oil and exhaust. Like you'd find in a parking garage.

Dunott was in or near the garage beneath McDougall's condo building. It was a guess, but a pretty darn good one, in my opinion.

I glanced at my watch. It was nearing 7:00 p.m., a reasonable time to expect an attorney to return home from work.

"Matt, we have to go to McDougall's condo immediately," I said after I'd released the spell. "I think Dunott might ambush him in his parking garage when he gets home. Do you have your gun?"

"Of course. I take it everywhere now. Even to the bathroom."

Before we left, I remembered to put my protective amulet back on. I needed all the tools in my toolbox to save my life.

CHAPTER 26
AIR AND EARTH

I knew the gate guard wouldn't allow us onto the property without someone authorizing us, so I parked at a nearby public-beach lot. We walked along the jogging path on A1A until we found a place to sneak onto the property out of view of the gate guard.

A powerful supernatural force was here. I sensed it as soon as I set foot on the grounds of the community.

A loup-garou, waiting for its prey.

The feeling intensified as we walked closer to the parking garage. The entrance was guarded by a gate arm, to be opened with a key card. I stopped as we approached it.

"Let's hide behind the bushes by the entrance," I whispered to Matt. "Dunott's in there somewhere, waiting to ambush McDougall. He'll smell or hear us if we walk in."

"I don't know what kind of car McDougall drives. How will we know when he arrives?"

"Good point. Let's hide near the other side of the entrance, where we'll have a better view of the driver. He has to lower his window to use the key card."

The waiting part was hard. We had no idea when, if ever, McDougall would arrive home. We weren't even sure that he wasn't out of town. All we knew was Dunott was here waiting, too, somewhere deep in the garage.

And who was I to say he wouldn't sense us and come out to get us?

I began to feel the unfortunate need to pee when headlights approached. It was the first car to come to the garage since we'd arrived. This exclusive community had only a couple dozen units.

The vehicle was a Mercedes, and when the window went down at the key-card sensor, McDougall's face appeared.

"It's him," I whispered.

After the car entered, we slipped past the gate and followed the taillights. The garage was one story, with several spots open. McDougall parked near the elevator.

Someone approached the car from the other direction, glowing yellow eyes piercing the shadows.

As I ran through possible tactics in my head, I lost a little confidence. The spells Angela had taught me were powerful, but they were crude and, well, elemental. What I needed right now was a magical net to drop on Dunott. How was a wind gust going to help me?

I gathered my energies and considered, then rejected, casting a protection spell around Matt and me. I couldn't afford to spend energy on anything other than putting Dunott out of action.

He came into view in the pool of light near the elevator just as McDougall was getting out of his car. Dunott was in his horrifying human-wolf hybrid form: covered in fur with a wolf's head but walking on two legs. McDougall hadn't seen him yet.

Instinctively, I cast my immobility spell. Even if Dunott could defeat it, it would slow him down.

He crouched, then froze before he could spring.

"McDougall!" I shouted. "Run! Go to your apartment, and lock yourself inside."

He glanced at me, then noticed the immobile monster for the first time. He darted toward the elevator bank. You're not supposed to take an elevator during a fire, but no one ever said you can't when a monster is chasing you.

I texted Angela, explained the situation, and gave her our location.

If you use your new spells, think out of the box, she replied.

"We need to capture him alive," I whispered to Matt. "Don't shoot unless it's the only way to save my life. And if you do, don't miss! We only have two silver bullets left."

"I'd rather shoot him now than wait until your head is in his jaws."

"You're too far away. You'd miss."

I walked toward the monster.

"Wait," Matt said. "What are you doing?"

I pulled from my pocket one of the tools in my toolbox. A long silver chain necklace. Draped over his head, it would greatly weaken him.

His wolf face glared at me, unmoving. I reached him and raised my hands to drop the chain on him. His eyes followed my hands.

Wait. His eyes shouldn't be able to move at all.

With a roar, he sprang at me, knocking me back with his human hands while his jaws opened incredibly wide.

As I stumbled backward, my back hit a car near McDougall's. The car alarm went off.

A gunshot rang out. Who knows where the bullet landed, but it wasn't in the monster's body. Great. Now only one silver bullet remained.

I spun to the side as the monster slammed into the car instead of me, thanks to the gunshot distracting him. Diving to the concrete floor, I tried to scoot under the car, but an inhuman hand grabbed my ankle, sharp nails digging into my flesh, pulling me away from the car.

Think out of the box, yeah right. I couldn't think at all. But I reached into my pocket and held the Red Dragon. As it heated, I focused enough to cast the wind spell. A microburst hit Dunott in the chest and pushed him backward.

Problem was, he still held my ankle, so as far as I might push him, I came along for the ride.

He lifted me by my ankle, and, from my upside-down position, I could only study his feet. I felt the cognitive dissonance of seeing a creature with a wolf's head and coat with a body that was shaped and moved like a human's.

I couldn't see his eyes, which I knew were those of an animal yet intelligent. But I got the sense that he was done with me. No longer did he need me to lead him to the were-wolves who had plotted against him. Now, I was nothing more than prey, a creature beneath him on the food chain.

His other human-like hand reached for me.

I fed more energy into my spell and sent another

microburst of wind that was so fierce and unexpected, he stumbled, backpedaling to keep his balance. His grip on my ankle loosened, and I fell to the ground.

I rolled away and sent another microburst at him. It knocked him in the shoulder and spun him around, but he kept coming, trying to dodge the gusts I sent. He was almost close enough to grab me.

Matt approached, aiming his gun with two hands.

"Don't shoot him!" I yelled. "I've got this."

"It doesn't look like you've got this."

"You're both dead," Dunott said. His distorted, growling voice gave me chills of horror.

He turned to Matt, as if he finally realized the human with the gun was more of a threat than the witch blowing air at him. He sprang without warning, swiping his hand-paw at the gun.

The gun went flying, clattering across the garage floor. Matt screamed as the other hand paw slashed him with its nails, shredding Matt's shirt from the shoulder along the back of his shirtsleeve. Blood gushed down his arm.

Matt turned and ran, but the monster pursued his slower prey. Another swipe knocked Matt sideways.

A thought came to me—you could call it an out-of-the-box idea. In the real world, wind generally blows in one direction at a time. But magic isn't the real world.

I concentrated all my power on the spell, sending a wind gust that knocked the loup-garou away from Matt.

But then I sent several sustained winds at the monster from every direction at once, hurricane-force winds. He was surrounded by winds coming from 360 degrees, and he couldn't move in any direction.

"Matt!" I screamed. "Get out of the garage, go to the car, and lock yourself inside until I get there. If Dunott comes to attack the car, drive away without me."

He hesitated, his eyes frantic, blood streaming down his arm.

"Go, now," I said. "There's a T-shirt in the car. Use it as a bandage."

The loup-garou roared with frustration and struggled to escape the winds that gripped him like a fist.

"I'm not done with you yet," I said.

Bringing all my concentration to the spell, I slightly lessened the intensity of the ones hitting his back, allowing him to back away. But they were still strong enough to prevent him from falling or turning around to escape in that direction.

As he continued to back up, he reached a concrete support wall, I adjusted the winds to pin him to the wall.

He howled in anger.

I walked casually toward the gun Matt had dropped. Picking it up, I pulled out the clip and checked. Yes, only one silver bullet remained. The clip slipped back in with a click that echoed against the concrete walls despite the wind noise.

I approached Dunott, aiming the pistol at his furry chest.

"Georgette killed your brother, didn't she?" I asked.

He growled and shook his head, trapped and unable to move because of the wind.

"It was all planned," I continued. "Your world was caving in on you. All the lawsuits and investigations into your criminal behavior. At first, it seemed like you were immune to everything. But then you learned federal prosecutors were about to indict you for racketeering. You knew the werewolves were plotting to kill you. In fact, their hitmen tried once, and others could try again. You decided it was time to bail out with a golden parachute—all those life insurance policies you'd purchased."

He growled, but his eyes revealed defeat.

"So, you invited your brother to visit from Canada. Then Georgette, who could handle silver bullets, shot him, and you put his body in your bed. Claude's DNA was the same as yours, so the authorities would be certain he was you. But just in case there were any mutations in his DNA that differed from yours, you burned down your own house to incinerate his body and destroy the DNA. Once everyone believed you were dead, you could punish your enemies and then live comfortably off the insurance money. It was a brilliant plan, except for one thing."

He whined like a dog.

"Yes, your wife was cheating on you. You didn't find out until after the murder, right? She was cheating on you with a human. McDougall, of all people. A guy who believed he was superior to you."

Dunott roared in anger.

"Yes, she murdered my brother," he said in his deep, thick voice. "I talked her into doing it. She made a big mistake, though. No one cheats on me. After I kill McDougall, I'm going to kill her, too. But you're going first."

He pushed forward, struggling against the wind, and I feared he was going to break free. I put more power into the spell. Then, I tried something very risky.

I began to cast the second new spell I had learned. I knew casting and maintaining two such strong spells at once required an inordinate amount of power and experience. I wasn't sure if I could do it, especially since these were new, less-familiar spells. But I had no choice.

Grasping the Red Dragon, I focused on both the air and earth elements, drawing the tremendous amounts of energy I needed from them as I watched Dunott getting closer to breaking free.

When the ground started trembling, it probably surprised me more than Dunott. The trembling became a rumbling and a shaking, making it hard for me to stay on my feet. Dunott, though, remained pinned to the concrete wall.

The vibration intensified. I could proudly say I'd created my first earthquake, as concrete dust sifted downward, and my view of Dunott became blurred. I was hoping a sinkhole would open and take him down into the bowels of the earth.

Instead, a *crack* came from above. And a chunk of concrete dropped onto Dunott's head, knocking him out cold.

Was he dead? No, I saw his chest moving from his breathing. Loup-garous don't die that easily. But since he was unconscious, he wouldn't be able to defeat my immobility spell. I cast it after I released the seismic spell but kept the wind blowing just in case.

My heart filled with relief when I saw the white van arrive from the Friends of Cryptids Society. Matt drove my car behind them.

"How did you get through the gate?" I asked Angela as she came to look at Dunott.

"I mesmerized the guard with a spell." When she saw my expression, she added, "I'm surprised you don't know a spell like that. I'll teach you."

"Well, here's your loup-garou in his hybrid human form. Be

very careful, because he's stronger than you can imagine. And you can't examine him for very long, because he must face human justice."

"Unlike werewolves, who involuntarily shift during a full moon, he'll be able to stay in human form while he's locked up."

"What if he shifts in order to break out?"

"The Society will make it very clear to him," Angela said, "that if he shifts in front of humans, we will put him down. Whether he's in prison or escapes."

"As long as I don't have to be the one who finds him if he escapes. How, exactly, would you put him down? With lethal magic?"

"It goes against my principles to use magic for killing. I have a firearm with silver bullets."

"You do?" I was shocked. "Mrs. Lupis and Mr. Lopez are against using silver bullets."

"Not once the loup-garou is properly examined and cataloged."

It sounded like my handlers would have rather seen me killed by the loup-garou than their precious monster being killed before their scientists got their hands on him. It was not a good feeling, believe me.

I put these thoughts behind me and looked at Matt's wounds. I made him stay in the car while I removed the T-shirt bandage and cleaned the lacerations with alcohol wipes from the car's first-aid kit. The wounds weren't pretty, but I didn't think they needed stitches. I applied clean bandages.

"Am I going to turn into a werewolf?" he asked, his forced bravado not hiding his fear and panic.

"Matt, you know you won't. He didn't bite you. The virus is in their saliva."

"Are you sure? How can you be so sure?"

I laughed. "I guess we have to wait to find out," I said, teasing him when I probably shouldn't have.

I sat for a while, just resting my hands on the steering wheel, trying to will my heart to slow down. My elemental energy had been drained, along with my innate energy. Replacing it was adrenaline from my fear.

Matt was staring at me. I looked at him, and he gave me the goofy grin I love so much. Here he was, all lacerated from claws, and he still had a sunny side.

"Can we wait a really long time before our next adventure?" he asked.

I chuckled. Then, impulsively, I leaned over and kissed him.

"Wow," he said. "That kind of thrill, I don't mind at all."

My NEXT, and hopefully last, task of the evening was to call Detective Shortle and fill her in on what I'd learned. I told her she needed to arrest Georgette for the murder of Dunott's brother.

"I'll make that decision myself with the D.A.," she said. "First, I'll bring in Mrs. Dunott for an interview."

Speaking with Shortle was like a splash of cold water to the face as I encountered the reality of the rest of the world. Meaning, most humans, those who didn't believe in the supernatural and, thankfully, had no reason to do so.

Explaining how I knew Georgette was guilty, I had to leave

out everything about werewolves, loup-garous, and silver bullets. Dunott's confession to me would be considered merely hearsay. And Ackney would deny what he told us.

I whined to Matt about it.

"Well, I'm going to write an article about all of this. I'll skip the supernatural stuff, but the story will be damning enough to embarrass the police and prosecutors into doing something. Being obnoxious gets results."

The same could be said for taking foolhardy risks to fight monsters. Well, maybe not. I'll let you know when my heart finally stops racing.

CHAPTER 27
NEW BOSS SAME AS THE OLD BOSS

My phone rang at 3:05 a.m. Through sleep-blurred eyes, I looked at my screen. The caller was Matt.

"Please don't tell me someone else has been killed," I said.

"Sorry, but yes," he said. "I heard it over the scanner. Greg Ackney found a body outside his apartment. I'm heading over there now."

That Ackney was involved meant this wasn't a random, unrelated murder. I reluctantly told Matt I'd meet him at the crime scene. He gave me the address, and I threw on yesterday's discarded clothes.

Ackney lived in a studio apartment that was the guest house of a home near his favorite coffee shop. I arrived to the now-familiar sight of flashing police strobe lights, solemn people standing around, and a body covered by a tarp. Matt was already there, speaking with Detective Shortle.

"It's a shame he won't face justice," she was saying to Matt.

She actually seemed happy when she saw me walk up to them. "Your leads were very useful."

"Thank you," I said. "But who is the victim?"

"Pierre Dunott," she said. "Not his twin. He has Pierre's ID in his wallet, and we've already run the prints. His were on file from a DUI years ago. And one thing about identical twins is they don't have identical fingerprints."

"How was he killed? Did it seem like an animal did it?"

"Bullet to the back of his head."

"Silver bullet?"

She smirked. "I'll let you know when we find out. I really wish we could have charged him along with his wife, but at least I feel confident she is going down."

"Really?"

"We arrested her earlier. Under interrogation, her friend, who had backed up Mrs. Dunott's alibi that she was out-of-town shopping on the day the brother was murdered, recanted her story. She wasn't with Mrs. Dunott at all that day. We even got Stuart McDougall to confirm many of the details. He knew all about the plot."

"Um, what about the others who were murdered?" I asked. "Do you have evidence Dunott killed them?"

"Not now. The medical examiner hasn't yet determined what weapon was used, or if they were killed by a human at all. The deaths look too much like animal attacks."

This was what I had been worried about. How the police in the real world would explain murders committed by a super-natural creature.

"Maybe they were animal attacks," I said. Matt looked at me strangely. "You know, there are people who keep dangerous predators like lions and tigers without getting them permitted. Animals could have escaped."

"I was thinking the same thing," Shortle said, though she didn't seem to buy it completely. But I had a feeling this would be the official explanation in the end.

"Thanks again for tipping me off to Mrs. Dunott," she added.

She stepped away to speak to a traumatized Ackney after Glasbag had finished talking to him. Matt and I walked back toward the street.

"How was Dunott even here?" Matt asked me in a loud whisper. "I thought the Society had him in custody."

"He must have escaped, because if they were finished with him, they would have delivered him directly to the police. I'm guessing he came here to ask for help from Ackney."

"And the Society shot him?"

I nodded. "Angela said she had some silver bullets, just in case."

"Wow. Do you think she did it herself?"

"I don't know," I said, though I was pretty sure she had. And it couldn't have been easy for her.

Later that day, I tried to call her, but she didn't pick up or answer my texts. While I was waiting for her to respond, I went to downtown Jellyfish Beach to see how the business owners were doing under the new regime.

"He's finally dead," Fred Furman said when I entered his boutique.

"How did you hear about it?" I asked. "It's not in the news yet because it happened so late, and the police haven't released any details."

"We know when our alpha dies."

"You know the loup-garou was Pierre Dunott and not his brother?"

"We didn't know. Not until last night when he was killed. It's sort of a telepathic thing, the feeling we get when our alpha dies. I put two and two together."

I filled him in on the other details, such as Georgette's role as the murderer of Claude Dunott and the plot to allow Pierre to disappear. Furman did not know any of this, of course.

"I feel lucky that I wasn't killed," he said. "I'd made it clear to Dunott that I hated him, but I guess he wasn't concerned about an old wolf like me."

I had come here to ask him about the werewolves' new fealty to my mother, but I didn't need to. The shop's door opened, and she walked in.

"Oh, look," she said, "two of my most loyal worshippers together in one place. Oh, wait. One of you doesn't qualify as loyal—or a worshipper."

"And someone in this room doesn't qualify as worthy of being worshipped," I said.

Furman looked at me in horror.

"Dearie," she replied, "when I'm through with you, you'll sacrifice yourself at my altar. Anyway, I was here to speak to Freddie. Some of your pack members are late with their dues."

"I'll strongly encourage them to make their payments," he said unhappily.

"Fred, are you the alpha of the entire pack now?" I asked.

"By default, ever since Dunott left the scene. I deserve to be, based on my wisdom and experience. Not to mention my leadership skills. But you know how it is. There's always some upstart who wants to challenge me."

"Like Maddie?"

"Yes. She doesn't enjoy being submissive to anyone."

"But you have leverage over her, don't you?"

"You got that right. The police would probably be interested in her having hired hitmen to murder someone, if I were to tell them accidentally."

Ruth hadn't been paying attention. She was browsing the overpriced cat-themed bric-à-brac and jewelry.

"I simply adore this platinum kitty paperweight," she said, showing Furman the piece that he had unsuccessfully tried to foist upon me. "I'd be honored to accept it as a gift."

"It's all yours, Saint Ruthless," Furman replied. "Enjoy."

"Thank you. I look forward to seeing you and your pack at the next worship service. And you," she said to me, "will visit me soon. Your deadline is rapidly approaching."

Her cocky expression both enraged and frightened me. Furman and I watched her leave the store and head to the art gallery next door, most likely to treat the owners the same way.

"That's six hundred dollars down the drain," he said bitterly.

"You were never going to sell that silly paperweight."

"You'd be surprised at the things people with too much money will buy. But this is unsustainable—this extortion and grifting. It's worse than with Dunott."

"She's an evil woman," I said.

"Someone should take care of her."

"Well, it won't be me. It's not in me to hurt her, even

though I'd have many reasons to justify it. But if someone were to find a way to drive her out of town, I wouldn't object."

Furman smiled and scratched a hairy ear. "I have an entire pack of werewolves full of ideas. Maybe someday, I'll share them."

"Make that sooner than later. I have a deadline coming up."

I ARRIVED at Squid Tower for the Wednesday night creative-writing workshop and saw Mathilda's hearse parked by the lobby door. Her coffin was in the back, suitcases stuffed beside it. I didn't know why a nun had so many suitcases when all she wore was a habit.

The thought crossed my mind that the luggage was filled with torture devices. That was a possibility I wouldn't rule out.

Mathilda and Agnes walked outside. I waved hello to them.

"You're certain you don't want to hire a driver?" Agnes asked. "We have a service that specializes in vampires. That way, you can sleep in your coffin during the journey."

"No," Mathilda replied. "I want to make it a leisurely trip back to New York. Take back roads. Stop in picturesque small towns. I'm hoping to find a place to move our convent. A place that's not as crazy as Florida."

Good luck visiting a small town in this hearse, I thought, and wisely didn't express.

"I'm so disappointed you didn't enjoy Florida," Agnes said, and anyone undead or alive could tell she was lying.

"Too many humans and vampires moving here. Too many

crazy politicians. I'm afraid there might be a movement someday to eradicate all vampires here."

"I wouldn't worry about that. Our politicians would be the last people to realize we have vampires in our midst," I said. "They have their own agendas."

"I remember all too well the periods in history when vampires and witches were persecuted," Mathilda said, looking down her nose at me. "I would be on alert if I were you."

"I always am. Well, I wish you safe travels." Agnes hugged her friend. "I'll miss you. We really must see each other more often than every century or two."

"Indeed, my love. Wherever we move will be in the Sunbelt, so the distance between will be so much shorter."

The two kissed cheeks and clucked like hens.

"I must be off now," Mathilda said, opening the hearse's door. "Thank you again, Missy, for fixing my tooth. It feels quite strong now, and I'll be careful not to bite any pearls or metal when I sink my fangs into someone."

I smiled and waved goodbye.

After the hearse drove out through the gate, Agnes turned to me.

"I'm not going to miss her one bit. I'm so glad she's leaving."

"Like I've said, people change over time. Especially if you're around for more than a thousand years."

"Not me, Missy. I never change."

In my mind, that was a good thing.

After the writing workshop, I finally got a text-message response from Angela:

The loup-garou was only the second cryptid I had to put down in my 37 years of being an enforcer. Dunott refused to be transferred to the police and escaped. When I attempted to recapture him, he tried to kill me. I realize now he would have been too dangerous to be in a correctional institution. What's done is done.

I got in my car and drove to Angela's house to be with her during this difficult time. She needed all the emotional support I could give her. And someone to sip Scotch with.

Oh my. How I disliked Scotch. But I cared for Angela too much to allow her to be alone.

Those of us who study monsters must take extra care to preserve our humanity.

PLEASE LEAVE A REVIEW

Dear reader, thank you in advance:
Please give my book a better chance.
Success and sales depend on you,
So kindly post a book review.

WHAT'S NEXT

Extracting a tooth fairy.

The crested mouth sprite, better known as tooth fairy to non-cryptozoologists, has almost never been spotted by humans. The exchange of cash for a baby tooth beneath a sleeping child's pillow is the primary evidence we have that they exist.

Leave it to a drunken Florida Man, passed out on the floor of his son's bedroom, to blow away the creature with his shotgun. There'd better be additional tooth fairies in the wild, or this means no more moolah for molars.

You know what's coming next, right? Yep, the Friends of Cryptids Society demands that I, humble witch and botanica co-owner, search for more crested mouth sprites. I must help the society estimate the species' population, as well as help capture one for scientific study.

Sure, no problem. Until additional bodies begin dropping.

And I learn that tooth fairies are a lot more complicated than we thought.

Welcome to Jellyfish Beach, a wacky world of murder, magic, and mayhem.

Get In Sprite of Herself at Amazon or wardparker.com

Sign up for my newsletter

Get a free novella when you join my occasional newsletter filled with updates on new releases, special deals, and amusing content. All you have to do is visit wardparker.com

Acknowledgments

I wish to thank my loyal readers, who give me a reason to write more every day. I'm especially grateful to Sharee Steinberg and Shelley Holloway for all your editing and proofreading brilliance. To my A Team (you know who you are), thanks for reading and reviewing my ARCs, as well as providing good suggestions. And to my wife, Martha, thank you for your moral support, Beta reading, and awesome graphic design!

ABOUT THE AUTHOR

Ward is also the author of the Memory Guild midlife paranormal mystery thrillers, as well as the Freaky Florida series, set in the same world as Monsters of Jellyfish Beach, with Missy, Matt, Agnes, and many other familiar characters.

Ward lives in Florida with his wife, several cats, and a demon who wishes to remain anonymous.

Connect with him on social media: Bluesky (@wardparker.bsky.social), Facebook (wardparkerauthor), BookBub, Goodreads, or check out his books at wardparker.com

PARANORMAL BOOKS BY WARD PARKER

Freaky Florida Humorous Paranormal Novels
Snowbirds of Prey
Invasive Species
Fate Is a Witch
Gnome Coming
Going Batty
Dirty Old Manatee
Gazillions of Reptilians

Hangry as Hell (novella)
Books 1-3 Box Set

The Memory Guild Midlife Paranormal Mystery Thrillers

A Magic Touch (also available in audio)
The Psychic Touch (also available in audio)
A Wicked Touch (also available in audio)
A Haunting Touch
The Wizard's Touch
A Witchy Touch
A Faerie's Touch
The Goddess's Touch
The Vampire's Touch
An Angel's Touch
A Ghostly Touch (novella)
Books 1-3 Box Set (also available in audio)
Complete Series, Books 1-10, Box Set

The Goddess's Daughter Urban Fantasy Trilogy

(Sequel to the Memory Guild Series.)
Of Envy and Empaths
Of Fear and Fae
Of Vampires and Valor

Monsters of Jellyfish Beach Paranormal Mystery Adventures

The Golden Ghouls
Fiends With Benefits

Get Ogre Yourself
My Funny Frankenstein
Werewolf Art Thou?
In Sprite of Herself
Worms of Endearment

www.ingramcontent.com/pod-product-compliance
Lightning Source LLC
Chambersburg PA
CBHW020047180626
46812CB00006B/2218